The Trouble With Gin

Betsy Katz

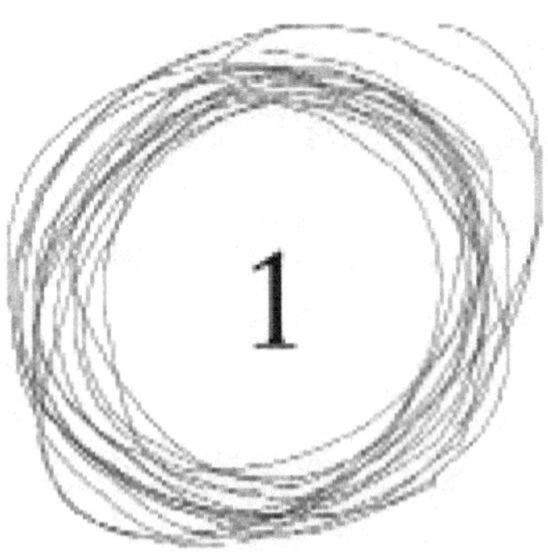

1

She struggles to remember any of the fading, hazy memories of the men who dragged her to this small, concrete, cell-like room. Her head aches and pounds from a drug induced hangover. She rubs her eyes as she lies on a metal bed that screeches at the slightest move.

She remembered a dilapidated motel room with turquoise and peach wallpaper with the sounds of TV static in the background. She had woken up from a banging on the door as it was broken down. She fought and yelled trying desperately to get away from them as they injected her with something that stung as it went into her veins and made the room blur almost instantly.

She fell to the floor, her vision going in and out and her ears ringing as the men bound her arms behind her back. She could taste sickening, metallic blood. She realized she was lying in a blood soaked carpet spot of an old motel. Why was there so much blood? She looked through the pool of dark crimson, where she fell on her face, toward the bathroom. Just before she blacked out she swore she saw a man lying face down. It looked like his leg contorted in the wrong ways while he lay in a pool of what she guessed was his own blood.

Gin shook her head and sat up trying to remember any details of how she'd gotten in that motel room. She rubs the spot on her arm that still stings from the needle. She can't remember anything else and her memory of what has happened is fading quickly.

In the dark room she could tell the concrete walls were stained from the floor up. The walls seemed like they had wisps of smoke creeping toward the ceiling. She starts to stand up, but the pain in her temples forces her to sit and steady herself before trying again.

Gin jumps as the single light fixture above her suddenly turns on, washing the whole room with a blinding, sickly blue hue. She shields her eyes as she struggles to stand, not sure what to expect next. There is a window with thick, stained, cream colored curtains on a wall beside her. She rushes over, clumsily and rips the curtains to the side. The window looks out to a red brick wall as far as she can see. Daylight shines from one side of the wall. She pushes her face against the cold wired glass to look out. There's brick as far as she can see in every direction. Just brick. Gin stands tall on her toes to see if there is a courtyard or anything at all below the window, but the wall seems to just go on and on.

A flash of memory makes her gasp and reminds her of the pounding on her motel room door. She remembers it burst open and several men broke through, yelling unintelligibly and forcing her to the floor. The floor was covered in blood. Why was there blood? There isn't any blood on her arms or chest now like there had been.

Gin feels herself with her fingertips, checking for any wounds. Her face isn't as tender from her struggle on the floor as she would have thought. Her arm is tender where she had been injected, but even that is fading. She isn't bleeding. She is almost completely sure of it. She convinces herself that she doesn't remember it correctly because of what they have given her.

She could see a small closet in the corner that was empty except for what seemed to be a blanket tucked into the top shelf. The concrete walls were covered in coats of various green paints; none of which seem to stick well to the walls. It's peeling like the fringes of an artist's imagination around the floor. Dark stains rose up the wall from the peeling paint in no particular pattern reaching toward the ceiling. Some places are solid putrid green and others have a multi-tude of disgusting stains that seem to have been soaked into the soul of the room.

A little square wooden desk is tucked into the corner of the tiny room with enough room for her to sit at. The desk has deep indentations along the sides where something had been carved into the surface. They're long and start at the bottom, moving up to the top in jagged gouges. The door on the other side of the bed is cold, hard, green metal that's scratched and banged up. Someone tried to get out before her. The door has rivets around the edges with a very small viewing window at the top. Gin slowly walks to the door, bumping her hip on the squeaky bed that sends shooting pain through her leg. She rubs the painful spot as she continues toward the large door.

Gin squats down below the window and takes several deep breaths before peering through the opening. She can't see much except the checked floor of a hallway and a light from somewhere in the distance that lights the hall. She reaches for the handle without taking her eyes off the window. The handle turns and with a deep breath she closes her eyes preparing to open it and face whatever lies on the other side.

She pulls the handle and the heavy door swings inward with a creak. Suddenly, she is met face to face with a very large man and a woman with deep smile lines. Gin scrambles backward, running into the metal bed that screeches at her mockingly.

The woman slowly steps toward her into the room with a tattooed man close behind. She pushes her glasses up her round nose and smiles widely.

"Hello Gin."

Gin feels a sharp shooting pain in her arm as the man jumps beside her. The woman continues, "Goodnight Gin. See you in the morning." Gin falls to her knees, then her chest and head hit the floor. She can't catch herself as she falls. She tries to yell, but a foggy blackness overcomes her.

She woke up to the overhead light beaming down on her deeply slumbering body, jolting her awake. She shielded her eyes from the light as she tries to adjust and wake up. A loud click-tok sound echoes through the nearly barren room, telling her that the door is unlocked. She rubs her sleepy eyes and tries to shake the remnants of what she barely remembers of a dream while still shielding them from the blue-hued fluorescents above. Her muscles are sore and there's a terrible pounding in her head from a medication hangover.

She swung her aching legs over the side of the metal bed which creaks as she moves. The floor is cold and hard under her toes. She stretches her arms over her head and arches her back while yawning. She is dressed in worn out jeans and a black V-neck tee shirt. She can see into the small empty closet. She rubs her temples as her head throbs.

She opened the heavy door. She could see an upper level hallway and a rail that overlooks a large living room area with couches
and tables. A tall slender man is also coming out of one of the doors
down the hall. He looks blankly at the floor as he drags his feet and
walks out of his room.

"Hello?" She says mostly to herself. He doesn't look up from
the ground, but turns around, grunts in a deep throat noise, and
walks back into his room.

Gin turned and walked to the right side where a metal grat-
ed staircase looms overhead of the living room area below. As she
continued down the sturdy stairs she can see a girl with long brown
hair in an over-sized thermal shirt. She sits in one of the navy floral
couches that are adjacent to more tables. Behind the tables is another rail-type wall separating another hallway of rooms. Gin has seen
around ten rooms, she figures.

In the common area sat a willowy mid-forties man on another couch, resting his head on the somewhat cushioned back of
the sofa. His hands rest next to the waist of his dirty white shirt. She
guesses he's looking at the ceiling. He seems to be looking through it.
His lip dribbles saliva to his chest.

Gin took her last few hesitant steps on the stairs and felt the vibrations of a door opening on the other side of the metal wall. A gate-type entrance noisily slid to the side letting people in the lower level out of the hallway and into the sitting area.

She quickly takes a seat on the far side of the room, by the windows. She sits, uncomfortably, at the worn, wooden table-for-two while rubbing her temples again. She wipes her tired eyes as if it would make the throbbing in her head go away.

More people stumble out into the room. She watches an older, slender man wearing a vivid velvety robe with matching slippers walk in. His shoulders slightly hunched forward as he makes his way toward another empty table. Another man wobbled to the couch next to the TV to watch Wiley Coyote chasing the Roadrunner. Behind him a lady in padded ankle shackles staggers her way to the closest chair and finds a great place to stare at the wall like the others. She giggles a few times and continues staring at the wall. Several other people sit around the room carrying on with what Gin figured are their morning routines.

So far she was invisible to the heavily medicated, ridiculous, people as they filter into the area and find their spots in various chairs and old couches around the room.

Gin turns her head, thinking she heard something whispered

behind her. No one was at the table behind her. No one. There wasn't anything but a worn, probably broken, table with a checkerboard painted on it and its matching pair of chairs.

"Gin, come with me." She jumped. A dark-haired woman holding a clipboard stood in front of the office wall with the door. "Well, come on. Gotta get you your stuff." She smiled as she motioned to go using her clipboard. Gin is certain it's the same woman as the night before.

Gin got up and walked across the room toward her, puzzled.

"My stuff?" The lady was probably in her thirties and definitely shorter than most. Gin looks into her eyes that sit behind green glasses, neatly on her round nose.

The lady answers, "Yea, the stuff you came back with." She wraps both arms around the clipboard and holds it in front of her silky blouse with delicate embroidery and matching pants.

Gin stands, looking at her. Her mouth gets dry as she stutters, "Back?"

The woman fans herself with the clipboard and held her smile. "Will you come with me please Gin?" It seems more like a demand than a question. Gin follows her into the office standing by the door. The woman closes the door. "Please sit down."

Gin crosses her arms. "I would rather stand. Thank you. What do you mean I'm back?"

The curvy woman sighs, replying, "Not here exactly. Your file says you were in the facility and now you're HERE." Gin's glare of disbelief made her shift to a monotone voice and she quickly finished, "I'm Head Nurse Bettie. This is your home for a while. Any further questions you can ask Dr. Veinkman."

Gin's arms shoot to her sides. She couldn't believe this crap. She yells at the so-called nurse, "What the hell is going on here?" After not getting a response she continued, "Where the fuck am I?"

Bettie writes something on a sheet and picks up her clipboard, clutching it as she stands up. She places her pen in the desk drawer, closing it. Keeping her monotone mood she responds, "You will have meals with the rest of this ward soon enough. You're allowed to use the common living areas when you're not in lock-down during mid-afternoon, then again at night. Group therapy is every afternoon and you are expected to attend and participate with the others. You will participate Gin."

Gin pushes her shoulders back, preparing to protest.

The heavy office door opened with a startling creak and a tall, large man stepped into the room, closing the door behind him. His head nearly brushes the top of the door frame. His arms are covered in black and gray tattoos. One seems to have a knotty tree on it with branches reaching toward his wrist. He clearly has more under the rolled up sleeves of his black button down shirt.

Head Nurse Bettie cuts Gin off as she explains, "This is our security personnel, Steve. Our rules mustn't be broken. He'll see to it that you understand." He nods at Gin as she continues, "He will explain the rest of what you need to know."

Steve motioned for Gin to follow. "Of course Head Nurse, I'll bring her up to speed." Gin stood looking at the behemoth of a man that she's being told to go with. She swallowed hard, wondering if he's the "shut-up and stop asking questions" kind of guy.

The head nurse waves with the clipboard and in a stern but perky voice adds, "I'm sure you'll feel right at home soon."

"Home?" She can barely muster the word. "You can't keep me here. No one has told me anything! I can't stay here my store needs me. Everyone's probably worried and wondering where I am."

The head nurse squints her eyes behind her glasses. "Don't worry your pretty face about that right now. This is a healing place. Talk to Dr. Veinkman about your questions. I don't have much information on your case right now." She waves with the clipboard again.

"See you soon child."

Apprehensively Gin replied, "Okay." She walked in front of Steve who is carrying clothes with one hand and opening the door with the other tattooed arm. He was absolutely the guy she remembered drugging her last night.

"Gin I'm Steve." She nods. "I'm going to go over the rules with you and give you a brief tour before taking you back to the common area. Let's get these clothes dropped off for you."

Again, she heard a hushed voice from behind her, "Don't believe him." She spun around and saw only the concrete wall of the office and a closed, dark grayish, green metal door.

Steve tilted his head to the side, "You okay?"

"I thought I…Yea, I'm alright." She shrugged her shoulders as she turned back around. Holy shit what was that, she wondered.

"This is an old building." He turned and walked quickly toward the rooms on the far side of the common room. "It has old settling noises and the pipes make noise sometimes in the walls. I don't think your room has them running through it, but you'll figure that out soon enough."

She quickly caught up to him as he continued, "We don't have that many rules, but it's very important that you, and everyone else, follow them so this can be a safe and healing place." He had a stern, gentle voice. "You are in WARD 27."

She gasps. "Twenty-seven? Of how many?"

"Forty-four." He pauses as he lifts his foot onto the bottom ridged step that led to the second level rooms. She knew he must be taking her right back to the room she was in earlier this morning. She squints as the blue florescent lights burn into her aching head.

He continues quite bluntly. "You are in Medium security. Some are Maximum security. I run them all."

Not trying to sound too defensive Gin asks him, "Why am I here? I need to get out of here. I need to go home." She had bitten her lip to the point of almost bleeding and mutters, "Why am I being kept here?"

Without acknowledging her questions, he turns and takes another step, "Be glad you're here. Dr. Veinkman and our staff are the best in the state." He loomed over her as they got to the top. They faced the room doors as he instructs her, "You're room one-eighty-one." She nods, seeing the people in the living room slowly funnel through a doorway underneath the stair way below her.

16

Steve looks at her intently. "Breakfast time. Everyone must leave the common area now. Your meals will be brought to your room for today. Then you'll have access to more facilities like the Café where you'll eat, the court yard, visits, and depending on the doc's recommendation you may be allowed outside on the grounds. That's right, play your cards right Jennifer and this will be a great place to heal and relax so you can get better."

"It's Gin not Jennifer. When can I call my family?" she barks at him, accidentally. Clearly he wasn't going to tell her why she was here at all. She worried about whether her boyfriend has a clue where she is or if her shop is alright without her. Her voice strains and she tries not to get weepy over her sudden homesickness. "I need to get home." She wanted to wake up from this awful dream and go home.

"Well Gin, you can't really do anything but group therapy, laundry, and shower for three days. If the doc says you can use the phone, then that's his call. Today you need to rest."

"Three days?! I have to let them know where I am. You have to let me call Joe." She felt her head throbbing as her heart pounded harder. "You can't keep me here. Let me out of here!"

He led her back to her room. "Does you no good to worry about those things. It'll all be taken care of for you. For now just get settled in and go to group therapy and get acquainted with your neighbors."

She felt the hairs on the back of her neck stand on end. The thought of getting to know anyone here gave her shivers. These people are crazy. Certifiably crazy. There was a person in shackles down there!

"Here's room 181."   He placed the stack of clothing on the wooden desk that had been painted so many times that it was rejecting the paint and peeling down the legs.

Steve turns and looks straight into her eyes from his towering position. His face becomes very serious. "We like to keep things nice and calm around here. If you have problems with that…well… We'll have to remind you." He laughs, a deep cackling laugh that made her uneasy. She shifts her weight as her stomach flops. He walks to the creamy stained window curtains and opens them, revealing a reddish-brown brick wall behind the thick wired glass of a window with no way of opening. Returning to his previously pleasant manner he continues, "It's not much of a view, but it's one of the few with some natural light." He looks at Gin and she forces a smile while he grins at her.

He starts toward the door, "Home sweet home. Everyone

here will help you heal, but if you start breaking rules, you'll have me to answer to."

She swallows hard and tries to not be intimidated. "I'm not going to break the rules."

He nods in approval. "Good. You will have to go to the common area before meals after your lock-down period is up. Everyone goes to the Café together and after breakfast you'll be able to go to the library once your three days are up. After lunch is group therapy. Most of this ward attends. It'll do you a lot of good to open up to everyone. Then there's lock-down till dinner. You can use anything in the common area during common area time."

She sighs and states sarcastically, "Seems like there's tons to do in there."

His smile fades. "Beats being locked in your room all day. I think you'll enjoy meeting the other patients."

She sighs again as he continues his speech, even though she kind of zones out because it's obvious he's gone through this a gazillion times.

"Keep your hands to yourself, keep your voice down, don't be a pain in my ass, and take your medicine when it's given." That is about all she gets out of his bullshit speech.

"Mmhmm. Got it." She knows she is a prisoner in a bizarre prison. "Speaking of medicine, can I get some Advil or something for this terrible headache I have?"

He nods. "I'll let the nurses' station know."

She gets a short tour of the laundry room, the bathrooms, the showers, and then they head back to the common area with her shoes flopping around. Truly curious she asks, "Where are the laces to my shoes? Can you answer that?" She has to be careful when she goes down the stairs not to trip.

He pauses and replies without looking at her, "You can't have weapons." He continues swiftly to the empty living room style common area.

Gin puts her hands on her hips. "What do you mean weapon? Am I supposed to strangle someone to death with a shoe lace?! You've gotta be kidding me."

Steve motions to a table by the railing. There is a steaming white tea cup sitting with a white paper napkin. "That's chamomile tea. Your lunch should be brought in shortly. You'll need to go to your room to eat it. I'll be in the office if you need something." He turns around and heads to the office behind him.

"Thank you...I guess." She talks to herself as he scurries

away.   She takes a seat in a wooden chair with a black vinyl padded cushion at a small round table with her tea. It is the only round table in the room. There are several larger couches in varying types of faded floral. Matching burgundy and green corduroy recliners sit across from a big boxy television that is hoisted onto a corner of the stained wall. It seems just out of reach. An arrangement of worn chairs and a sofa sit around it. There are four more tables all mix-matched, but made of roughly the same dreary, dark-colored wood. Each set with at least two chairs.

She stares at the steam that rises from the earthly scented tea in front of her. She picks it up and feels the warmth of the glass on both palms as she inhales the soothing vapors. She closes her eyes and takes a sip of the hot liquid. It has a hint of honey and does actually help her calm down. Gin looks at the yellow tea as she enjoys the moment of quiet. She needs answers, but this quiet time soothes away the tension somehow.

She jumps as she hears her name from the top of the stairs. "Gin?" She looks in the direction of a man's voice. "Your food is on your table upstairs." A man with a red Hawaiian shirt peers at her from a railing.

"Thanks.", she calls up to him.

"No problem-o." He walks away down the hall as quickly as he'd come.

Gin carries her half empty cup of tea up the stairs to room 181. She apprehensively steps through the large metal doorway into the room. On the small desk sits a tray with a plastic plate of scrambled eggs, an apple, a box of cereal with a milk carton, and plastic ware. She sits down and picks at the eggs, which aren't half bad. At least they're not starving her to make it easier to brainwash her, she thought.

3

A loud knock on the door and a loud clank of the door lock bring Gin back slowly from her peaceful nap. She really hoped it would have all been a dream when she awoke. She enjoys being asleep much more than the reality of being in what she assumes must be a mental ward. She pulls the covers down from over her head. She's unsure when she got into bed.

Steve peeks his head through a crack in the door before opening it entirely. "You have an appointment with Dr. Veinkman. Get yourself together and meet me in the common room so I can take you to see him. Nurse Bronson may be waiting for us."

Gin rolls over toward the door and props her head up on one elbow. "Alright I'll be down in a minute."

He leaves the door open as he heads off down the hall. She gets out of bed and runs her fingers through her hair before using a pathetic comb to finish the job. She figures she should look halfway presentable to meet the Doctor, even if she does feel like her eyes want to roll into the back of her head. Maybe he will be able to give her some answers.

She pulls on her lace-less Converse sneakers and works her way down the hall and down the stairs, sitting on the first available seat. Steve is nowhere to be seen, so she sits still trying to wake up completely while she waits. She notes that she seems to stay in this twilight place somewhere in-between awake and asleep.

Other so-called patients sit around in groups talking amongst themselves. There are five people sitting in the room with her. An elderly man watches an old western on TV with his eyes glazed over and glued to the television making sure not to miss a second of it. A scraggly grayed woman and a man of around Gin's own age seem to be having a very in-depth conversation. The man she talks to rubs his chin, deep in thought for whatever they are talking about.

One patient looks longingly out the window, focused on something with his chin held high and a cup of tea in his hand. All his fingers embrace the cup, except his pinkie which he raises as he sips from what is probably drugged tea. If not, Gin is almost glad these people are heavily medicated. Another lady walks around the room talking to the man at the television occasionally, then would walk away and talk to herself then walk back to him with loud thumping steps and seemingly answer him then continue to carry on a conversation with herself. He looks directly at the TV, never uttering a word to her.

Gin looks around to see if Steve or Bronson are around to take her to see the doctor yet. They aren't. She guesses they are busy with a patient. She is sure people here can be a pain at times.

After a few minutes, the patient at the window casually walks beside her table and with his pinkie in the air and his navy leisure suit on asks, "You're getting settled in, I presume?"

Gin looks at him blankly, "Yeah I guess so. As much as I can, considering the circumstances."

As if she hadn't replied at all, he introduces himself, "I'm Alfred Willscott, and you may call me Alfred. Banana gram. Welcome to the Spookatorium. I trust you're finding the place rather welcoming."

She offers a hand but he steps back, taking a long hard look at her hand as if she offered him poison. Reluctantly he steps forward to her and lightly grips her hand in a friendly, yet hesitant shake.

He pulls his hand back and wriggles his fingers in front of him. "It's a beautiful day, wouldn't you say?"

She figures she should go along with him rather than upset him and nods. "The Spookatorium?" Shivers run down her spine. She isn't entirely sure she wants to know why they would call it that.

"Hi Alfred, I'm Gin. Nice to meet ya. Would you like to give me a tour of this wonderful facility here?"

He cuts her off, "Of the Spookatorium?! Oh my! Where to begin..." he looks around the room with a puzzled look across his face.

Gin pipes up, "Yeah we could start our tour anywhere. Oh I know! I'd really like to see the door. Or maybe the end of this hall over here?"

Alfred blinks slowly and looks puzzled. "Hello. I'm Alfred. I'm not sure if you have noticed but my friend, George, and I are going to start a deeply moving movie." He points to the TV and the scraggly old man smiling wildly and waving his hand madly without lifting it. "What's Eating Gilbert Grape. It'll be starting anytime now. You should join us. George believes you will enjoy it."

Gin moans deeply realizing how little help people around here are. She runs her fingers through her hair before asking "What's this Dr. Veinkman like anyways? Is there anything I should know?"

He straightens the already neat neckline of his robe and then wiggles his fingers around as he speaks. "Ah yes, you want to know about the Doctor. I first met Dr. Veinkman after my little accident. He came to me in the hospital. It was almost a magical moment really." He looks longingly into space as if remembering some amazing dream.

Gin raises her eyebrows. "Accident?"

Alfred looks confused. "No,no, there's no accident here… wait YES!" He pointed his index finger and his eyes got wider. "I was mugged on my way to work, you see. Lousy, damned bastard whacked me on the noggin." He points to his bald spot then returns his lanky fingers to wiggling in front of his chest. "I had forgotten many things and Dr. Veinkman came banana gram! to me in my greatest hour of need. It was his decision to let me live here, you know." He shrieks, then returns to his high-pitched, upper class ramblings. "He is wise in his ways, though we don't always agree. I'm sure that's common among brilliant minds." He smiles with his chin held high. He's the only one around here that I find trustworthy. I suppose Steve too." He winks at Gin. "Well, the staff anyways, but that's our little secret."

Gin winks back while giving him a quick nod, "Okay." She knew he was incredibly unstable, but he seems friendly enough. He obviously took quite a blow to the head and it probably contributes to his erratic behavior. That would absolutely explain the completely folliculary challenged spot on his head. She props her face on her elbow, not sure what he may say next.

Alfred stands up straighter and continues to sip the tea that Gin knows must taste horrid. She may even smell the poison in his drink. Hers smelt nothing like that. He sits down at the table with her, setting his half empty cup down gently. "Shall I have them fetch you some tea, my dear?"

She shakes her head, "Oh no, thank you. I'm good on that." She holds her hand out in front of her and shakes it, no. She looks over her shoulder to see if Steve has returned yet, but he was still nowhere in sight. "Have you seen Steve or Bronson lately? I'm supposed to meet them here to go see the doc."

Alfred crosses his arms and rubs his chin. "I haven't seen them since this morning. Of course I wasn't looking for anyone until now." He smiles with his pearly white teeth. Gin notes that they are so perfect they probably weren't real. He leans in closer to her. "I could try to summon him if you wish."

Gin smiled slyly, "Really? How would you do that exactly?" She crosses her arms and tilts her head to the side.

Alfred stands even straighter and raises his chin. He wiggles his fingers in excitement. "Oh it's simple really." He raises one hand, palm up in front of his face. "I call upon the same universal powers that are healing me, for which I am exuberantly grateful." He clears his throat before continuing, "I summon thee, Orion's belt, to bring to this wonderful friend of mine the handsome, youthful nurse that she requests! Bring forth Bronson or Steve so that she may continue on her destined path to see the glorious Dr. Veinkman!"

Gin's jaw drops as Alfred speaks. He seems to have announced the arrival of the wizard of Oz in front of the pearly gates. She quickly shut her mouth. "Umm. Thank you Alfred, you've been a great help." He returns his "on-my-honor" upheld hand to his side.

He clears his throat again and in a serious tone squeaks out, "You're very welcome my dear. The universe has many powers, you must first learn how to harness them and appreciate them." He smiles at her then sips his tea, both hands wrap around it. He closes his eyes as he enjoys it.

From the office Bronson calls to her,"Gin are you ready?" It startles her and she turns to see him walking toward her.   "Y e s , I'm ready." She looks back at Alfred who gives her a wink and waves goodbye before returning his attention to his tea.

Nurse Bronson wears a bright blue shirt. Gin figures he was

the one who gave her dinner. She stands and follows Bronson as he motions to her. He smiles showing bright white teeth that contrast with his tanned skin. He obviously took care of himself. His dark hair is flawlessly spiked forward and she could tell that he is quite muscular for being so slender. He leads her to the door under the stairs where everyone had left for the café yesterday. There is a long hallway with a few heavy metal doors and at the end are closed double doors. He finds the correct key on his keyring and sticks it in the single hole on the door, then pushes the metal bar, opening one of the doors. "Have you seen the doctor yet?" His voice is calm.

She shakes her head as she replies, "Not yet." Gin looks at the name tag with a black and white photo of him that hung from a blue lanyard around his neck. "Why does that say Shannon?"

He laughs as he leads her through the doorway, locking it on the other side. He blushes slightly. "That's my last name. When I transferred to this ward they messed it up. Security's supposed to get me a new one. Steve's too busy to check on it." He takes a couple steps down the hallway with the checkered black and white tiles. "This way." They pass a room with no doors that must have been the café, with brown picnic bench style tables that are empty. They come to a door with a silver knob and stop. He knocks quietly before opening it. "Gin is here to see you, sir."

From the other side of the door a deep calm voice answers, "Great, thank you Bronson."

Bronson steps to the side and opens the door all the way. "Here you are."

Gin steps into the large room as the door closes behind her with a click. She wonders why there was no lock on this door like all the others. The room has warm brown walls that are lined with oak bookshelves full of colorful books. A silver picture frame sits on one of the shelves with a photo of a black dog in it. Degrees from six or more colleges and universities line one wall, all in dingy silver frames.

Behind the large solid, heavy desk sits a large balding gray-haired man in a black pin-striped suit and a shamrock green tie. One hand wears a gold wedding band and the other wears a gold and onyx pinkie ring. He smiles warmly. He looks nothing like what she pictured. She was really hoping for Bill Murray.   "Hello Gin it's nice to see you. I hope you're getting settled in."

She shrugs her shoulders. "I guess." Gin takes an upholstered chair in front of his desk. The plaque on his desk reads Dr. Veink-man, Ph.D.. "I don't understand why I'm here."

He folds his large hands together. "You're here to heal, Gin.

Nothing more. What do you remember exactly?"

She pushes her hair behind one of her ears and grips the arms of chair. A deep frown tugs at the corners of her mouth. "I..I was sleeping at some motel. Something woke me up and I was..." She trails off. "There was all this blood coming from somewhere. I think there may have been someone else there, but I don't know who. I saw a huge puddle of blood."

She sits and stares at her lap for a moment trying to recall what she could. "Some guys broke in and put a bag over my head and dragged me away. The next thing I knew I was here." Her forehead wrinkles as she tries hard to think. "I want to go home." She holds back the tears that swell by her nose.

The doctor unfolds his hands, pushes his leather chair from the desk and stands up. "I'm sorry it was so unpleasant. You were taken to a freshly cleaned room though." He walks to the window to her left, looking out it. "And what do you remember before that?"

Agitated, Gin tries to control herself from tearing up. "This is ridiculous, I should be home. I need to let everyone know where I am. That I'm okay."

He looks at her and raises one eyebrow. "Where exactly is home Gin?"

"Brooklyn. I live in Brooklyn. I have a book store in Manhattan. I need to get back to my shop! My boyfriend must be trying to find me. I need to tell him where I am." She forces back the tears that are swelling in the corners of her eyes.

Dr. Veinkman walks back to his desk and opens a manila file folder. "You don't need to worry about that. Your friends have been informed where you are. They know you need to get better Gin."

Frustrated, she grips the chair tighter. "Why does everyone think I'm sick?!? I shouldn't be here! I'm being forced to stay." Angry tears start to run down her cheek which she quickly wipes away with the back of her hand.

He looks at her with sympathetic eyes. "It's true that you need to stay here. This is a very healing place and I'm confident that we can get to the bottom of your troubles. It will take time Gin."

She wipes another tear from her face and angrily yells, "I shouldn't be here. Those people out there, THEY should be here." She pointed to the door. "I don't belong here. I'm nothing like them."

He nods. "Each patient has their own individualized medical plan. You're not like many of them, I know. Still, you're here because you need to be. I expect that therapy will become very beneficial for you." He sits down in his rolling, padded chair.

Growing impatient Gin sits up straighter. "There must be some kind of mistake! I don't need to be here. I didn't get a bump on my head and I don't mumble garbage to myself." She feels her blood pressure rise. "I'm cured from whatever you think is wrong with me. I'm not sick, okay? I need to go home!" She feels her heart start to race as the muscles in her neck tense and she can feel a headache coming on.

He wraps his fingers around each other again. "I realize you're upset, but I think you'll find it welcoming here and you can begin to heal and get better. You can get some much needed rest too."

Trying not to yell and make matters worse she squeaks out, "I don't need rest. I need to get back to my life. My shop risks being closed for good and I've worked so hard to keep it open in spite of losing so many customers. They can't possibly be expected to take care of everything without me."

He takes a controlled deep breath and replies, "You shouldn't worry about anything. Everything is taken care of while you just work on yourself right now."

Gin takes several heavy, deep breaths and fights back more tears. "I just want to go home. Please let me go home." She stands up and impatiently slams her hand on the front of his desk.

Choosing his words carefully Dr. Veinkman replies, "This will be your home for right now. I understand you're upset and confused." He returns his attention to the chart on his desk.

He picks up his shiny pen that has spots of wear from years of use and jots something down on the manila folder. "We'll work together to get you healed and safely on a path to recovery. We'll have group therapy later today and everyone will be there. Please try to calm down before then. Everyone here has the right to a safe healing environment. We'll talk more again soon." He presses a button on the intercom next to him. "Bronson, Gin is ready to go." He returns his attention to Gin. "You'll be alright, you're perfectly safe here. I promise you that."

Before she has a chance to protest, Bronson opens the door. "Come on Gin." He motions for her to follow him again.

Gin finds it hard to control herself as she pleads with the doctor to let her go home. He looks at the file folder and writes something in it without looking back up at her. Bronson holds her arm and leads her out of the room back into the sterile hallway and closes the door.

Gin pulls her arm from his grasp. "I can walk myself thank you." She glares at him then starts toward the double doors. She stops at the doors waiting for him to unlock them and turns to face him, still glaring. "Why won't anyone listen to me?"

He shrugs his shoulders as he unlocks the door. His keys jingle as the door opens. "The doctor's orders are the doctor's orders. He's only doing what he feels is best for you."

Gin huffs and follows him through the doors and back toward the common area door. "When can I use the phone?"

He continues walking. "I'm not sure, but probably after your lock-down period is over. I don't know for sure. That sort of thing isn't up to me. I'll let Head Nurse Bettie and Steve know you'd like to make a call though." He turns and smiles at her.

Even though she is upset his warm smile seems genuine and melts away her anger. She can't help but smile back. "Thanks."

He opens the door that leads her past the Café and several closed doors to the common room. "You can go ahead and go to your room. Your dinner is waiting for you."

Gin rolls her eyes "Oh joy," she sarcastically replies in a dry tone. The common room is empty except for a young cleaning lady who was vacuuming the stained, light-turquoise carpeting.

Gin bats her eyelashes and asks, "Can't you join me for a little while? I'd really like the company." She turns to see him already steps away with his back to her. She slyly eyes the key ring that hangs from his belt and smiles cunningly.

As he turns she can see that Bronson's face has turned bright red. He clears his throat and sternly says, "Gin you need to go to your room now. It's lock-down. I'll be by later to check on you when I do my rounds. I'll bring your meds then and take you to group."

Gin huffs and rages off toward the stairs. He watches as she stormed up them. He follows her long enough to see her walk down the hall to her room. "Enjoy dinner," he adds in a pleasant voice.

She huffs loudly as she walks through the door and plops herself down on the bed. Its springs echo throughout her small concrete room. Gin finds her dinner on a brown tray with a tan cover over the contents. A milk carton, an orange, and plastic ware sit next to it. She pulls off the cover to find a compartmentalized plate with green beans, applesauce, turkey dinner with dressing covered in gravy, and two Oreo cookies. She sighs as she throws herself into the plastic chair and picks at her meal.

From behind her, she hears a whisper of a voice say, "Don't trust them." She turns to see an empty room behind her. The pipes here sure are weird. She eats the fruit and green beans then places the cover back on the tray.

She climbs back in bed and covers her head to block out the luminous lights. She pulls the scratchy white sheet up in frustration. Being asleep seems like a fantastic escape from the depression that is starting to set in. She has no idea why she is being kept here and everyone is acting like there's nothing wrong.

She heaves a giant sigh and says to herself. "Why am I here? Why can't I go?! I just want to get out of here." She rolls over onto her side and starts to let go of the stinging tears. "I...I...I want to go home. I just want to get out of here." She kicks her feet around in frustration, throwing her body around on the squeaky bed. She tangles herself in the scratchy sheet causing her to get more upset and thrash more. Gin finally closes her eyes and lets her sobs get lighter and lighter until she slowly sobs herself to sleep.

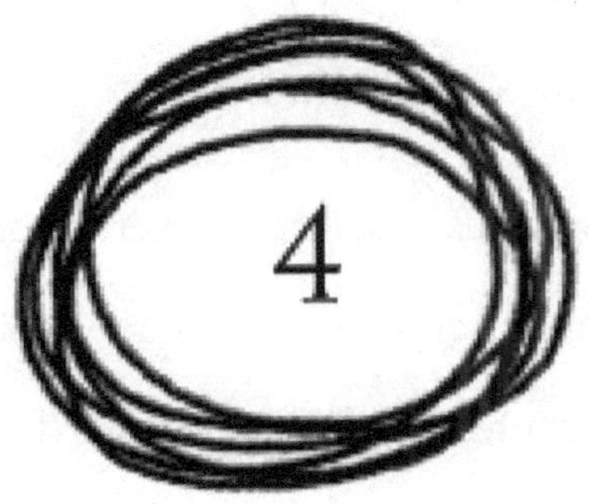

4

So far Gin has walked unnoticed through the common room filled with around fifteen non-coherent people. She finds a seat at one of the tables that has her name handwritten on a folded note card. She sits on the plastic chair with a hard, curved seatback. A white tea cup is sitting next to her name. She stares into the steam, looking through it.

She sighs heavily at the thought of going home. Her lip quivers slightly as she sniffles quietly, trying not to draw attention to herself. She wraps her arms around her chest as a little shiver crosses her body. She can't imagine staying here long. The other people are most likely completely incompetent in getting out of here.

From over her shoulder, making her jump, Gin hears, "It's chamomile tea. Supposed to be calming or some crap." Gin turns around in her chair. A blonde guy about her age, smiles from the floral couch behind her. A dark-haired girl sits hunched over beside him, scribbling feverishly on a piece of paper. Her white knuckles hold her pencil as it races across the page under her brown hair. Her face is mostly blocked by her straight locks.

"Good to know." Gin casually answers back in a monotone voice. She looks back at her cup and wraps her hands around it. Her fingers tingle at the warmth. She holds it to her face and closes her eyes, breathing in the steam.

The guy gets up and sits next to her at a chair with a flop. He scoots his chair closer to her. Gin's face twists into an irritated half smile as the attractive stranger leans in closer to her. "You're lucky it's not drugged like Alfred and George's there." He nods toward the dirty haired man with his back to them on a sofa across the room.

Gin makes a disgusted face as she looks at the table in front of her before looking back up to her company. Quickly she wraps her hands around the hot cup even tighter than before. She knew his drink smelt different.

He laughs casually before adding, "I'd think that he'd really dislike the bitter tasting tea, but they tell him it's just imported salt water and it's not supposed to be delicious to be a treat." He looks intently at her. "I'd really like to help you if you'll let me." She shifts further from him as he nonchalantly smiles at her.

"I'm Gin." She wonders if there is going to be an end to his company.

"Yea, we know who you are. I'm Luke… in case you didn't know. How are you today?"

Gin crunches up her nose at the statement, and then shrugs it off. "Yea, whatever." She isn't in any mood to start an argument with anyone kept here. After all, these people were likely to say anything. She should just expect it. "I'm fantastic." She looks around the dimly lit room, her eyes drawn to a pacing scraggly-haired woman at the side of the room with obvious signs of a hard, worn-out life. Her hands and feet are restrained by sweat-stained, creamy padded cuffs attached with links of chain running between them. The matching tightly strapped bindings make it seem that she could sit comfortably at the table. She doesn't sit though; instead she paces, mumbling under her breath to herself.

The woman walks in front of an older man that Luke had pointed out, with very dirty, long patchy hair facing the opposite direction on a sofa. As the pacing woman turns around in front of him and starts her return trip, the man bounces giddily on the old springs on the sofa, clapping wildly. He giggles several times as she passes. She walks several feet and turns around to repeat the whole process again. The man again bounces like a small child on the sofa as she passes him. Gin's eyes widen as she shifts uncomfortably.

She turns her head back toward Luke, still intently watching the scene thirty feet beside her. Gin asks quietly, "Why is she restrained like that? Seems hideously barbaric and cruel."

The girl who had been scribbling on paper spoke up, making Gin jump visibly. "Cause she's bat-shit crazy. Talks to herself all damn day." She doesn't look up from her page but continues to dig her pencil into the paper in front of her.

The dark-haired girl looks straight at Gin and sarcastically says, "You're not blind are you? If it's not obvious why, you need to see the shrink more often than Annie does."

Gin meets her gaze sternly and replies defensively, "I'm not blind. I don't see anyone else tied up like she is. Sorry that I asked why she's more qualified to wear those restraints than the others."

Luke pipes up, "All right now. Let's all just agree that she's right where she should be. He relaxes in the chair crossing an ankle across his knee, propping his arm on the back of the chair and adds with a chuckle, "I am, however, due to get my release papers any time now. I'm not crazy." He let out a boisterous laugh.

The girl gets up slightly to swat him hard on the shoulder. "I'll believe it when I see it." She shakes her head and rolls her eyes.

Gin focuses on Luke. "How are you getting out?" Without

waiting for his response she adds, "I have to get out of here. I need to go home." She adjusts herself in the hard chair.

"You and me both!" the girl laughingly says. "I've been trying to get out of the Spookatorium for a while now, believe me."

Luke interjects cynically, "Maybe if you didn't try so hard to get out you would, Marie."

She continues as if he hasn't said a thing. "They always seem to know when I'm trying…"

Gin cut her off abruptly, "Did you say the Spookatorium? What the hell kinda name is that?"

Marie replies in a very fact-of-the-matter tone, "You said you aren't blind, but have you actually looked around this place? Not much warm fuzziness going on." She waves a finger around the room as she speaks. She points to Annie and George. He seems to have intense ADHD and dementia. He pauses his bouncing just long enough to let Annie pass him again with her blank glare and mumbling.

Luke looks at George and his clumpy hair. "You know George likes you, don't ya?"

Gin feels a sour flop in her stomach looking at the ridiculousness on that tattered couch. "I'm not sure how to respond." Her voice trails for a brief moment. She returns her attention to Luke and Marie.

He explains, "He doesn't warm up to everyone."

Marie adds, "He's harmless. It's not the residents you have to worry about anyway."

Luke's voice grows strict. "Don't overreact Marie. The staff isn't that bad."

"Whatever," Marie says under her breath, "says the guy who supposedly doesn't have to deal with them much longer." She laughs, hard.

Marie relaxes again and asks, "How are you today Gin?"

Gin narrows her eyes looking at Marie, unsure how or why she knows her name. Why would she ask how she was? Why did Luke? She doesn't know these people. Realizing that news probably travels fast in here she replies, "I'm good, considering I'm being held as a second rate citizen. You?"

As soon as the words left her mouth she wishes she hadn't asked. She purses her lips in an emotionless non-smile, looking around the room.

"I'm good today." Marie stretches her arms up past her ears and then crisscrosses her legs, leaning back comfortably. She suddenly scoots to the front edge of the couch and gazes into Gin's eyes, making her uneasy; then lets go abruptly, returning to her position on the overstuffed couch with her paper and pencil.

Luke laughs. "I'm good too. Slept great. That's one thing that I can say I've had since I got here. I'm going to miss that when I leave. You can't get any peace in the City."

"You're leaving? How are you getting out of this place?" He suddenly became more interesting.

He smiles an ear to ear grin. "Hell yea, I'm done in a couple days. I'll be stalking the streets in no time." He laughs. "It's not that bad here. Everyone's cool for the most part." He shrugs his shoulders. "Unless you're a bitch to 'em of course."

She leans in a little closer and in an even more hushed tone says "I'd do just about anything to get out of here and go home, personally."

He shakes his head. "I was just telling Marie to stop thinking and talking about getting out." He twitches his head sideways a few times and continues, "It's really not a big deal. Go to their stuff and try to actually listen to them now and again. Blah Blah Blah. You'll figure out their system."

"What do you mean? You're saying that I should just stay here and do what I'm told to do?!" Gin squints her eyes and cocks her head to the side. "Listen, whatever your name was, I shouldn't even be here. I'm being held prisoner. I can't even talk to my family!" She turns from him and crosses her arms around her chest. "There is NO reason for me to be here."

He laughs casually. "You and Marie there, both could learn to relax." He motions to Marie. "Maybe you guys could start a meditation club?" He swipes her shoulder playfully with his hand.

"Huh?" Gin stares at him with absolute disbelief that he could possibly be considered sane by any means. Gin's eyebrows raise and her shoulders go back as she replies, "I don't believe I'll be staying long enough to be starting any club. Sorry." She looks at the girl who has finished mutilating her paper with the pencil and now stares at the page. Her head hung low and a pool of her hair piled on the arm of the sofa.

"Hey Marie. You done?" The guy looks at Gin with a smile then turns toward the girl. Again he asks, " Marie, you done writing in your diary?"

Nothing. Marie sits motionless staring at her finished page in an eerie expressionless gaze while her lower lip droops.

Luke explains, "That's her thing. She'll be fine. She'll be back to her quirky self soon like nothing ever happened." Gin looks at Marie as her eyes stare unfocused on the page in front of her. The gleam in her eyes is fading.

"She doesn't respond at all?" Gin tilts her head to look at the blank shell of a woman that now sits on the couch. Just moments ago she was a snappy sarcastic thing.

Luke, in his cool manner replies, "Nope. She can't hear you or see you. She's suspended there in some sort of trance. She'll usually snap back and pick up right where she left off." He shakes his head and looks at her sympathetically. "Sometimes she doesn't though. I don't know if it's seizures or what. The nurses just leave her be until she comes around." He laughs before adding, "She doesn't know when it happens. Sometimes it's just a minute or two and sometimes it's a really long time. I can hear her yelling when she's been taken to her room while she's down for the count."

Gin wraps her hands in a tight ball in front of her. "I have to get out of here. There's been a mistake. I'm not supposed to be here." Her lip quivers. "I have to find a way to tell Joe I'm in here." Her voice shakes as she speaks.

Luke interrupts her, "Hey now, it'll be alright, Gin." He pats her clasped hands for a brief moment. "How 'bout this. If you haven't gotten a hold of your Joe before I leave, I can look him up for you when I get back to the city. Tell him where you are." He hands her a napkin and gets Marie's pencil. "Write his info down."

"Oh thank you!" she scribbles on the napkin trying hard not to tear it. "Here."

Marie snaps her head toward him. "It's not a diary Luke it's a JOURNAL." Her voice was irritated. "Diaries are for those pansies that write down their feelings and their boohoo hoos about their pathetic lives." She pushes her dark hair away from her face and turns her attention to Gin. "I write my dreams down before I forget them. I bet you don't do that. Soo… shut the hell up."

Gin shakes her head, her eyebrows raised in disbelief of what is going on. She tries sitting up straighter. "I never remember my dreams." She laughs. "I'm not sure I even dream anymore."

Luke says, "Everyone dreams, just 'cause you don't remember it doesn't mean it doesn't happen."

Marie turns her legs facing them on the sofa. "And some of us wish we didn't have them."

Luke widens his grin and looks right at Marie and says, "See

Gin, you guys could learn to relax."

5

A knock on the door followed by a deep male voice calling her name wakes Gin up. "Gin it's time to get up. I have your medicine."

She rips the covers down wondering when she went to bed and sees a large man with a blond military style haircut peering back at her. "I'm Dale, the nurse on duty tonight. Bronson had to leave early. Here's your medicine." He walks to her bed and offers a small white cup and a cup of water. She reluctantly takes the pills and washes them down with the water. He checks her mouth to make sure the contents are gone. Seeing that she has taken the pills he replies in a deep, calm voice, "You have five minutes to go down to the common area and I'll take you to group."

Gin hands him the cups back and in a whiny voice says, "I don't want to go anywhere with those people."

Dale laughs. "Everyone has to go to group. You're no exception. You have the chance to share with the group and work with the doc. I'll see you in five minutes downstairs." He turns and leaves, his sneakers making a squealing sound as he heads down the hallway.

Gin gets up, wrestles her shoes on and sits on her bed for a moment. She sees a cherry-wood box sitting on the desk and walks to it, noticing decorative cut-outs along the outside. It may have been hand-carved. She runs her fingers along its edges before opening the gold colored latch. Inside the box are several postcards. She thumbs through them and finds an older looking faded one with a picture of the space needle in Seattle and flips it over to see if it is signed by anyone. 'Talk to you soon' is written. There's no signature and it isn't addressed to anyone. She pulls another postcard out with a picture of waves and the inscription of California in colorful print on the front. She flips it over. It reads 'See you soon.' It also has no return name and hasn't been addressed to anyone. Strange, she thinks, these are strange.

She puts the cards back in the box with the others, planning to inspect them further later. She re-latches the small box and sits it on the desk.

She makes her way downstairs, again noticing that her head is in a fog. She stumbles over one of the stairs and catches herself on the metal tube railing. She steadies herself and continues down to the common room. She takes a spot next to Marie on a couch and looks at her scribbling away on a piece of paper. Marie looks over at her and asks, "What's another word for happy?"

Gin thinks about it for a moment and responds, "I don't know, um… cheerful, delighted, joyful?" She watches as Marie scribbles on her paper with a tiny yellow pencil that has no eraser as she smiles happily with her choice of words.

Other patients sit around the room doing their thing. George smiles a playful smile while humming some unknown tune. Alfred is longingly looking out the window even though it has no view. Annie is talking quietly to herself, occasionally looking at the elderly patient next to her and perhaps talking to him. He stares at the floor, never responding to her. A very large man and a skinny older woman with scraggly white hair watch T.V. with their backs to her.

Gin rubs her hands together, takes a deep breath and lets it out slowly. She squirms on the couch trying to get comfortable. She turns to Marie. "Whatcha working on?"

Luke steps toward the girls and replies, "A page in her journal." He takes a seat next to them.

Marie looks up for a split second, "They only give me one damn page at a time."

Gin frowns, "Why's that? Seems silly."

Marie doesn't look up. "I don't know, guess they think I'll paper cut everyone to death or some shit." She makes a thrusting knife motion in the air with her pencil, giggling high pitched sound effects as she does, "whet whet whet." She can hardly keep her laughter in. She returns to her writing, still smiling.

Gin laughs at the thought of it. The three of them sit, giggling, as Dale walks from the office into the room. "Alright everyone. Let's go to group." All the patients stand up and shuffle their way to the door under the stairs.

George skips and Annie walks with her ankle restraints toward the door. Gin notices Annie was more sluggish than before. She follows as the other eleven or so people make their way through the door to the hallway. They enter a door on the left, before the café.

There are several red and blue plastic chairs sitting in a circle. Gin rolls her eyes, taking a long calming breath, then takes a seat next to the fat man she'd seen earlier watching TV. He was sweating profusely; she tried not to notice. She tries not to look anyone in the eyes and stares at the floor. The rest of the patients find their seats. George stands in front of Gin and in a nasally voice says, "That's my spot."

Gin looks up at him and answers in a wavering voice. "Sorry I didn't know."

George giggles to himself and turns away from her. "That's okay Gin, you couldn't POSSIBLY have known that I'd like a break from it anyways. It's too confining and judgmental." He staggers away from her smiling.

Gin watches as he takes a seat next to Alfred. "Uh okay. Thanks… I think."

Dr. Veinkman walks into the room after everyone has found their way to their own hard plastic chairs and takes his seat in the remaining chair. "Hello everyone." He holds a single sheet of paper. His chair seems quite small for such a large man. Gin realizes that his tie seems to match his bright green eyes.

Steve enters the room, closes the door and stands by with his big tattooed arms crossed with sort of a scowl across his face. He silently stands by the door like a soldier.

"Hello." The room full of people echo back to the doctor, almost in unison.

Dr. Veinkman looks at the paper he holds in his large hand then looks up at the patients. "We have someone new with us today. Some of you may know her. I'd like everyone to welcome Gin. Please make her feel at home with us here."

The room fills with clapping and a reverberation of "Hello Gin!" from all around the room. After everyone else has stopped George continues to clap gleefully for a moment.

The doctor nods and continues, "Today's topic is how to express your emotions correctly using WORDS to let people know how you feel." Gin rolls her eyes and thinks this has to be some kind of joke. He points to a chart filled with smiley faces showing different emotions and goes on, "So Annie let's start with you. How are you feeling today?"

Whatever Annie is doing in her head stops with an obvious suddenness and she turns her attention to him. She whines, "I feel blurry."

Dr. Veinkman nods his head. "Okay. Okay. Is there anything you'd like to add?"

"NO. Just blurry."

"Alright Annie that's a great start. We'll go with that today. George, how do you feel today?"

Marie blurts out, "Like a wind-up toy, obviously." She crosses her arms and huffs a piece of hair out of her face. Luke puts his finger to his lips, telling her to hush. Gin tries not to laugh.

George bounces in place and claps his hands. "I feel pretty, oh so pretty. Also I feel…happy." An enormous smile fills his face and his eyes bulge from their sockets. He stares at Gin, making her uncomfortable. She squirms in her seat hoping he will look away sooner than he does.

The doctor nods again in approval. "Good George; that's good. Ben how about you? How do you feel today?"

The fat man next to Gin takes a breath, thinking about his answer. He forces a smile. "Um… I feel joy and joyness."

Dr. Veinkman smiles. "I'm glad to hear that Ben." He looks around the room. "Alfred how are you feeling today?

Alfred sits with his chin held high and replies, "I think I'm feeling sad today."

The doctor squints his eyes and looks at him sympathetically. "Why do you feel sad today?"

Alfred gets more comfortable in his seat, thinks about it for a moment and says, "The trans-dimensional energy from space is keeping me from being happy. I know that the stars are lining up and giving their signals to Banana gram! the atoms in my brain so that I know what I must do." He holds his fingers to his head like antennas and moves them around while looking up at the ceiling.

Dr. Veinkman studies him for a moment, not at all shocked in what he'd said, then replies, "I'm sure it's going to work out fine for you. If you want good things to happen in your life, you must be certain you will receive them."

Gin feels sick to her stomach. The room starts to spin as she braces herself with the sides of her chair and tries hard not to let anyone else know. How could she be here now? This can't be real. She fights back the urge to vomit, then feels a little better. He vision is spotty and her ears start to ring.

The patients' voices sound like they are coming from the other end of a long tunnel. She starts to hear them as background noise. She hears the doctor's voice call her name. It's as if his voice is in slow motion. She turns her attention to him and with all her might blurts out, "I'm frustrated that I'm here and being kept so medicated."

She doesn't hear his reply. The words he says slur together and don't make any sense. Gin feels the room spinning and closes her eyes for a few moments.

When she opens her eyes she sees the room of people sitting in their chairs. They look normal for a moment and then their faces begin to change. She looks at Alfred. His chin is starting to sag as if it were melting. She looks at Luke. His nose and cheeks are sliding down his face. Her heart starts to race as she looks at Marie whose chin and cheeks are stretched out at least five inches below where they should be.

Gin shakes her head to try to clear away what she is seeing. It couldn't be real, she thought. Voices are slowed down and she can't understand anything that is said. Her head droops as she closes her eyes tight. Her stomach is churning.

"Gin? Gin?" She hears the Doctors voice and opens her eyes. "Are you alright Gin?"

She shakes her head. "No." When she opens her eyes she sees the doctor just as he should be. She looks at the empty chairs around her. No one else is there.

Dr. Veinkman looks back at her concerned. "Group's over. Why don't you go back to your room? You look like you could use some good, restful sleep." He looks up at Steve. "Help Gin to her room?"

"Of course sir." He moves calmly toward her, dwarfing her as she sits hunched in the chair. Gin runs her fingers through her hair, scratching her head as she does.

"Rest. Yeah, I need to rest." Sarcastically she replies, "seems like all I do is sleep." She gets up from her hard plastic chair, stretching her back. Steve helps her walk slowly back to her room as she stumbles and uses him for support. She is so dizzy. "Thanks." She says to Steve.

Steve helps her to her bed. "No problem. Good night Gin, the nurse tonight will check on you later. I hope you feel better when you wake up."

She hopes so too.

She rubs her eyes, yawns, and wonders what has just happened. She knew what she saw couldn't be real. Maybe she fell asleep during group and dreamt some horrible dream. Her stomach didn't feel sick anymore, but she couldn't shake what had just happened. She slowly feels her thoughts fading and her eyes getting heavier. She doesn't fight dozing off.

The light buzzes on above her, making her awaken from the fog that filled her head. She lay in bed, in her room. She tries to rub her eyes and shake her sedated sleep away. She can't raise her arm! She lies on the bed restrained, pulling and tugging with her arms on her padded wrist restraints. She tries desperately to kick at the tighter padding around her ankles with no success. Her head aches and she wishes she could reach a sore spot on the side of her face. She tries to remember the details of the night before.

The door slowly creaks open and Head Nurse Bettie enters through the crack. Her forehead is wrinkled above her brow and a disappointed frown stretches across her face. "Good morning Gin."

Still trying to shake the deep sleep she'd been in Gin replies, "Maybe your morning has been better. Doesn't seem so good." Chuckling and looking up at the white padded restraints around her wrists. They are attached to her bed with leather straps. "Let me up." She flails her arms, making them swing a little.

Nurse Bettie squints her eyes and frowns, making an almost fish face before snapping back to her usual unnerving, plastered smile. Nurse Dale steps into the room behind her, pushing a metal medicine cabinet. He stands beside it and fumbles for his keys before pushing the metal door to the side. He leans his shaved head into the cart and fumbles for medication.

"You need to calm down Gin," Nurse Bettie replies. "You've had a rough night and you really should get some rest. The Doc says you're going to stay here until you have calmed down. Dale will take good care of you," she finishes. She hastily spins around and leaves the room before Gin can respond.

Gin squirms and shakes her restraints. "What gives you the right to tear up my life? I'm not an animal!" Her voice growing scratchy as she raises it to a yell. "I want the fuck out of here!" The bed shakes as she wrestles her bonds.

Dale keeps his cool, mellow voice, "You're going to get through this Gin. It's not healthy for you to fight so much…relax." He holds a white paper cup to her lips and slides his hand behind her head, lifting it to the cup. "Here's some water. You must be thirsty."

"Uh huh." She sips hastily and gasps after finishing. She hadn't realized how thirsty she was. He lays her head down. "Can I have more?"

He turns to the cart and retrieves a carafe of water that he refills the paper cup with. "Of course." She eagerly lifts her head for liquids, as he lifts her to reach more comfortably again. "I have your meds here too so you can rest.

She sobs. "I want to go home, I want Joe. Why can't I go home?!?" She wrestles her restraints, rolling left and right. It was useless, she wasn't going to get out.

Dale holds out her cup of pills. Now her voice was shaking. "I...I don't want them." She turns her face away from him as she cries.

"You need your rest Gin. Doc's orders. You have to take your pills. I don't want to fight with you over it."

"I don't want them." She shakes her head and sniffles. "I don't want to rest!" Gin wriggles her body this way and that. She gasps in pain as she turns her wrist too far in the restraints. Feeling defeated, she lays still and tries to catch her breath. A deep frown crosses her face.

"You done? You're really not helping yourself right now. Let me help you out, will ya. You have to rest so you can calm down and get out of this room sooner." Dale reaches out to help her drink again and places the pills in her mouth as she tries not to choke on the poison. She swallows the pills, drinks the water, and rests her head back on the pillow with a sigh.

"I hope you feel better tomorrow Gin." Dale slides the cart door closed with a screech, locks it, and pushes it into the hallway outside. Its wheels echo in the nearly barren room. Gin stares at the ceiling, she didn't want to think about tomorrow. She wanted this terrible dream to end and for her captors to set her free. "Get some rest. Tomorrow is a new day, full of new possibilities." Gin continues to stare up as Dale slips out the door and closes it behind him.

It didn't take long for Gin to start feeling the effects of the medication. She was already groggy, but now she felt her eyelids get heavier and heavier. "Let me out of here." Gin cries to herself. Her voice bounces around the room. She sniffles and cries out, "Let me go. Somebody help me PLEASE." She sobs and wrangles about, trying to free herself. It's no use, she thinks. They'll never let her go. She knows that no one here intends to help her. She has to try harder to get out first chance she has. She takes a deep breath and cries out with her voice quivering and cracking, "I want to go home!"

She starts to breathe faster as she realizes the pills are making her dizzy and the room starts to buzz around her head. The single bulb above her seems to pulse with her heartbeat. She wrestles with her wrist restraints again. In a slurred high pitched tone she pleads for them to let her go, but no one hears her cries for help. She sobs loudly as she desperately tries to stay awake and conscious.

Gin cries as she tries to free herself. The padding burns around her wrists, rubbing her skin raw from fighting the leather so hard. It doesn't budge, but she takes a deep breath and with a loud grunt she tries one more time. Her back arches up as she yells out in frustration at being tied to the bed. "Let meee goooo!" She feels her lips start to tingle as her head swims. She relaxes and cries silently to herself, scared of what might happen to her next. Her body shakes as she cries harder. "Why won't you help me?"

She feels her body getting heavier and heavier as the drugs make it difficult to think or see clearly. She watches in horror as the light above her pulses from a bright, clear light, to a fuzzy darkness. She struggles to keep her eyes open. She looks around the empty room as it spins wildly around her. She attempts to pick up her head to keep from falling asleep, but her neck isn't strong enough to even make it budge.

Her heart races as she battles to stay awake; she has to free herself. Her face feels warm as her ears buzz and hum. She fights to stay conscious. She can't move her legs or arms, they feel heavy and uncoordinated. She opens her mouth to scream, but only a quiet gasp escapes her lips. Tears stain her cheeks as she stares hopelessly toward the ceiling hoping someone will help her get out of here.

She wants to be home with Joe and Brinkley. She knows he must have told the police she was missing. They must be trying to find her. She has no way to let anyone know where she is. She cries harder, hoping Joe will find her before they can hurt her. She knows that he would be worried, and she pictures him sitting, hunched over on the edge of his chair. His face washed with worry lines and dark circles under his eyes as he chews on the side of his finger like he did when he asked her out for the first time. She had spent so much energy showing him that his corporate way of thinking could shut out all of the local family owned businesses. He hid the truth about his family's business to try to protect her from the ugly truth about his family. It wasn't personal, it was business. She swears that if she hears that from one more person she's going to scream. Maybe even kick them.

Though their relationship hadn't started off well, they were practically inseparable once they got through their differences in business morals and ethics. Joe had tried so hard to impress her with his fresh flower deliveries and stopping by when she was sick. He had become her best friend, the one she could confide in. She missed him and shudders at the thought of never seeing him again.

She cries harder, yanking hard on the restraints, making the bed squeak as she struggles. She gives her wrists a couple more yanks before relaxing them above her head. She feels vulnerable. "Why are you doing this to me? Please let me go! Please. Please let me go." She mouths the words but no sounds come out. She doesn't understand why her hands are above her head. Don't most restraints end up by the sides, she thinks. She moves her lips, begging to be set free again. Nothing comes out.

She fights to keep her eyes open, unsure what may happen if she loses consciousness. The light buzzes in her head and a humming pulses behind her forehead as the lights fade in and out. Gin opens her eyes as wide as she can and lifts her head off the pillow to try to fight the overwhelming sleepiness coming over her. "You can't do this. Let me go!" Her voice starts to trail as her slurred words fall on deaf ears. Her head falls, as her muscles give out, making a thud on the pillow that shakes the screechy bed.

Her eyes begin to close and she struggles to keep them open. She can't focus on anything further than her face and she knows she can't fight it much longer, but she is determined to stay awake. Her eyes slam closed for the final time. The muscles around her eyes start to relax and loosen. "Let mee go! AAAAAAAhhh! Someone helppp meee!" is all that escapes her throat.

She thinks of walking in the park with Joe and Brinkley as

her body relaxes and stops responding to her demands. For a moment, she can feel the soft coat of her dog brushing against her leg and hear Joe's warm laugh. A slight smile reaches crossed her face before being overwhelmed by the sedation, falling into a deep sleep.

7

The pipes somewhere in the wall make a sort of hissing and clanking as she listens to the sound of her own heartbeat growing stronger. The sounds jolt her awake. She feels her raw, throbbing wrists still tightly bound above her head, and her back feels sweaty. The pipes groan down the wall then clank above her head. She tries to look around the darkened room, groaning in pain as she stretches.

"I can help you…if you want it," says a hushed, strained, and almost quieter than a whisper voice from the corner of the room. Then there was silence. Gin's eyes bulge as she holds her breath to listen. The pipes rattle somewhere just beyond her room.

She is frozen as she tries to calm and catch her breath as she looks out the corner of her eyes. She doesn't move a muscle. There is no one there. Not anything except a desk and crappy chair. She must be going crazy. Her imagination is playing tricks on her. They have given her so many drugs that the life and the love that she has fought so hard to get back is getting blurry. Just like the ceiling above her. If they have drugs to make her sleep, why wouldn't those people drug her and cause her to freak out too? She relaxes her stiffened muscles and silently curses the head games they're playing on her. There's no telling what these sick people will do.

Without warning she starts to twist to free herself, huffing and puffing in the empty room. Her ankles are bruised and swollen along the top of her feet. They burn and pulse in pain as she twists.

"Oh Joe help me. Help me!" She gasps as she chokes back tears, but they soon consume her. She sobs as she pleads, "Help me, somebody help me. I just want to go home! Please…PLEASE!"

Her hair begins to fly wildly as she thrashes around. "Let me the fuck go! Let me the fuck out of here!" Pain shoots through her wrists and she screeches. "AAaagh." She continues to fight and yell. "I want out of here. Let me go!" Her wrists stop her from moving around. They are tender and rubbed raw. They are moist and sting where the restraints are rubbing the skin away on the sides. That's where she feels most of her weight when she pulls. She rests her head back on the pillow and cries.

She is weak and struggling is beginning to be excruciating where she is bound. Her neck and back are fatigued and her shoulders feel as though they were propped above a fire, and roasted a nice golden brown.

Whispering from somewhere by the door, a scratchy hushed voice startles Gin. "You can't believe them." Gin shakes her head to dislodge the tricks her own mind is playing on her. She looks at the ceiling and tries to think of something calming. Anything that doesn't remind her of the torture she was going through.

Her chest rises up and down as she fills her lungs with relaxing breaths. She thinks of how she always enjoyed her walks in the park. The warm sun on her freckled cheeks and the crisp Manhattan air always reminded her to slow down and enjoy the evening. Her favorite part of the day was when the sun was just starting to set and the buildings in the background cast the most amazing silhouettes as she pulls her sweater tighter for warmth.

She thought of the birds in the park. She hopes she will see another bird. She hadn't really cared for them before, but she can hardly remember what they sound like now. Brinkley would chase after them, surrounding them both in a cloud of pigeons, feathers, and dust. She and her furry friend would meet a tired Joe at work and walk home together in the brisk evening air, hand in hand.

She sighs as another pipe creaks somewhere in the wall pulling her from her lovely walk with Joe. Then she hears it again in the ceiling. The moans above her head are like the pipes are sighing after feasting on the nothing in the wall. The rumbling noise subsides, so she closes her tired eyes and dozes off and on thinking of her beloved book store that she hopes to see again. She is too weak to try to struggle to free herself and lets the waves of sleepiness take her over as the pipes fade in and out of the background.

The pipes shake in the wall loudly, next to her head, bringing her eyes back into focus. She watches the wall out of the corner of her eye. The dark concrete bounces muffled thuds around the cell-like room. Suddenly, she feels a drip on her face. Startled, she shakes her head, 'Augh'. Another drop hits her face, this time closer to her eyes. "Augh, no" She starts to panic that there might be a leak in the ceiling. "Someone help me!"

As she begs for help the drops continue to spatter on her face and neck. "Someone help me PLEASE help me!" She screams out in panic, the drops getting more frequent and her neck becoming soaked from the mysterious liquid. "Nurse! Somebody help me! I need help! Oh My god help me!"

The liquid pours from the ceiling. Slow at first, then a couple of spurts covering her forehead and chin. A few random drops fall then it stops briefly. She tries to catch her breath. Some of the liquid runs down the side of her lip, warm and tasting metallic. Blood. There was blood in her mouth! The ceiling continues to drip as she thrashes around so hard she nearly moves the bed. She screams in disgust and fear. "Blood! No, No, NO. Oh my god help me!"

The voice from just below her feet this time whispers, "You're not safe, you have to let me help you." Gin barely hears the voice through her struggling. This can't be happening.

She fights to keep the blood from pouring into her nose and mouth as she yells for someone, anyone, to help her before she drowns in the putrid liquid that keeps falling from above her. She thrashes as she is covered in the sticky liquid that pours over her like a burst artery.

"AAghh! Ahhhghh!" She screams a blood curdling scream while kicking and struggling to somehow get free. She was getting dizzy again and the sickening feeling of panic was making her woozy. She suddenly started seeing stars as she realized she could choke tied to this bed. Her face thrashed side to side for every breath.

She was having trouble breathing now, spitting the thick blood from her mouth as she fought to catch her breath. She couldn't get her face away from it, she was starting to cough and breathe it in. "Helllpp Meee!" She desperately cries for help, gurgling sounds escaping her throat as she tries to scream. Her muffled cries for help become quieter and quieter.

Gin lays choking on the blood dripping from the ceiling, gasping for breath. She flails helplessly, bound in the bed. Her lungs burn from inhaling the rancid liquid. Her body leaps forward in an effort to get air before thudding hard on the mattress and being still. Her head falls to one side, eyes wide open, and she can't fight the feeling to sleep any more. She tries for one last big gasp of air but it doesn't come.

"Gin wake up."

Gin springs awake, gasping, sitting straight up in bed as if an alarm had gone off. She reaches around her neck and feels her face as she chokingly tries to catch her breath. "There's no way that was a dream" she says aloud. She pats her shoulders and feels her throat.

She rubs around her sore wrists, now free. She lies back down, relieved that it had all just been a really bad dream. She rests her eyes for a moment, feeling grateful for waking up from that awful dream. There are no restraints. Her heart is still racing from her horrifying dream.

"Gin wake up. You have to wake up."

Gin opens her sleepy eyes and looks around the room. It was dark and only a little light from somewhere down the hall shone through the tiny window on her door. She seems alone. No one is talking to her. She rolls over and pulls the warm covers up to her neck. She knows she had heard her name. So sure that it had woken her up. She felt her mind must really be drugged up, she was having horrific, lucid dreams and hearing things. She has no idea what they've been making her take.

She lays with her eyes closed for several minutes, trying to go back to sleep. She takes soothing breaths to try to relax her body and mind back to sleep. She had almost dozed off again when she hears a low, crackly voice from somewhere in the room.   "Gin wake up."

Her eyes grow large as she sits up to look around the room. She knows she heard it this time. "Is someone there?" She can't see anyone in the room with her. No one in the dark.

Again, a raspy voice repeats, "Gin wake up." She freezes as she looks in the direction the voice had come from. The closet only has hangers and her clothes folded in the top compartment. She can see the back of the empty closet.

Hesitantly, she calls out into the dark. "Who's there?!?"

She pulls the covers back and throws her feet over the side of the bed. Her feet on the cold floor, she slowly walks to the door and looks out the tiny window. Only a slight light from down the hall, three or maybe four rooms away. No one was there.

86

"I'm your friend Gin. I want to help you, but you have to wake up."

Gin walks toward the closet, where the voice seems to come from. Her feet are startlingly cold from the concrete floor. She wishes they would turn the heat up at night. A shiver runs up her spine and she rubs her arms, wrapping them around her. "Why can't I see you if you're my friend?"

She gets to the closet and starts to examine it. Dark and empty, just as she thought it would be. She waves her arm around the emptiness of the closet, banging hangers around and into the wall. She pats the fabric on the top shelf and reaches around behind them. She turns back to the bed when she is satisfied there is nothing inside. "How're ya supposed to help me?" She climbs back up onto the bed. Sckweek-ricka-ricka the metal bed echoes around the room. Her eyes adjust to the light slightly as she becomes more awake.

The voice is a slither of a whisper by her ear. "They are going to take him away."

Gin jumps and turns her whole body on the squeaky bed. "AAhg! What? Who?" No one is next to her.

There is silence as she looks feverishly around the room. "No. No one's gonna get taken away in the middle of the night."

The voice becomes harsher and strained, as if standing in front of the door and yelling a calm whisper, "Luke is going to be taken away. There is nothing you can do to help him. You can only help yourself."

Uneasy, Gin looks around the room. "Who?...Where are you?" She's positive there's no one else in the room with her. She gets up again and walks to the door. She feel around the edges of the cold, hard metal door. She reaches to see further down the hall through the little window. Only lights down the hall somewhere.

As she looks out the tiny window, lights start flickering in the hallway. Soon it is completely illuminated but she can't see anything except the tile floor in either direction.

The voice sounds as though it's next to her ear again, "They're going to take him away. No one can help him."

Gin shakes her head in disbelief. "No. That can't be true."

The voice cuts her off with its raspy, edgy sound, "It is true! They're going to take him away for good. Shhhh."

A couple of orderlies that she doesn't recognize come walking down the hall. They're dressed in blue scrubs, like some of the patients, but theirs are newer and clean. They each wear a white medical mask that straps behind their ears. She hasn't seen anyone before that they resemble. What are they doing?.?

She quickly ducks so they won't see her. Gin remains hunched down for a moment then peeks back through the door. Nothing but floors and suffocating green walls. She can hear yelling from a distance on the other side of the door. Gin bites her fingernails as she looks through the tiny opening.

The Voice comes from the closet again. "I'm sorry there's nothing we can do. He didn't help himself." Before the voice can finish, Gin can hear growing howls and noise from down the hall. Banging makes her strain to see through the window by her head.

The noise and yelling grow louder. She can't make out the sound, but there's an orderly in the distance. The yelling is muffled by the door, becoming clearer. Luke's voice yells out through the hallway, "No! Leave me alone. You can't do this to me! STOP!"

Gin watches in horror as the two men drag Luke out of his room and down the hallway by the shoulders. He yells at them, fighting to free himself from the restraints he is confined by. His normally large body is being dragged like a ragdoll on his back. His hands are bound in front of him by his waist. Zip ties bind his wrists. His legs drag and kick as they pull him past Gin's closed door. She stares in disbelief and fright as she instinctively beats on the door with her fists. "No! Leave him alone!"

They don't look at her or even notice her. They robotical-ly drag Luke, twisting his body to free himself, past her door. Her mouth gasps as they pull him backwards and seated on the floor by the shoulders. They flip him back over almost in unison, onto his back when he struggles enough to rotate. His face is twisted in hor-ror and covered in sweat. He frantically tries to free himself of their grip. He throws his head violently. The orderlies silently grab him and pull him further down the hall. His feet sprawl in an attempt to stop himself.

He yells repeatedly, as he thrusts his shoulders to get away. The men silently regain their grasp and continue dragging him.

Gin makes her hands into fists and pounds on the door yell-ing, "Let him go. Let him go! No! You can't take him away!"

She watches him disappear out of view in a matter of seconds as the orderlies seamlessly take him away. She hears him yelling and fighting through her door, now further away. The lights in the hall flicker again then turn off. Now only a little light shows in the dis-tance. Her heart races as she jumps up and down trying to see down the hallway.

Gin pounds on the door a few more times and then falls to

her knees on the floor. With her hands against the door, she rests her forehead on the cold, hard metal, and cries.

She cries for what seems like an eternity; until she can cry no more. She climbs back into the bed and covers her head. She lies silently, unable to muster anymore tears. She hopes for sleep to come quickly.

9

Gin lies on her bed staring at the ceiling. Her brows wrinkling as she tries to wrap her head around what has happened to Luke. Her eyes are sore from crying the night before and her nose is stuffy and plugged.

Marie quietly walks to her door, knocking on it as she pushes it open further. "Gin. Can I talk to you?" She stands in the doorway in sullen silence, looking at the floor.

Gin nods her head and sits up to face Marie. Both girls have dark circles around their eyes. Marie moves closer and takes a seat on the bed next to Gin.

Marie looks down not making eye contact. She look at her feet and she looks at the bed, but not at Gin. Her forehead is worried. "I...I don't know what to do." Her voice is unsteady.

Gin tilts her head and pulls her legs closer to her body. "About what?" Marie looks like she feels about the same way today.

Marie sniffles and slowly starts, "They took Luke and I don't know how to find him." Her eyes swell as she looks at the wall.

Gin sits straighter. "You saw that? I thought I was the only one who saw that."

Marie shakes her head several times. "They took him. They took him away." She wipes her eye with a wrist then looks toward Gin. "I'm afraid I'll never see him again."

Gin talks in a loud whisper. "I saw them take him too. Where do you think he is? Who took him?"

Marie shakes her head again. "I don't know." She looks at Gin with her bloodshot eyes. "They don't ever come back Gin. Luke's never going to come back. I don't know what to do." She shakes as she speaks.

Gin tries to keep her voice genuine and asks, "Didn't he say he was leaving? Could it have something to do with that?" This is no time for jokes, but she doesn't know what to say.

Marie yells a loud whisper, "NO. This isn't like that. He isn't the first to leave. They don't come back." She shifts uneasily and looks toward the door then back to Gin. "I'm afraid I'll never see him again."

Both girls sit in silence for a while as Gin tries to understand what's going on and what happened to Luke. Marie quiets her sniffling as her breathing flutters. It is a relief that Marie saw it too, but it was even more unsettling that it hadn't been a dream. What could have happened to Luke? Why was he taken the way he was? She has even more questions than just a few moments ago.

Marie stands up to leave quickly. "I'm not supposed to be in here. They'll be angry if they find me in here. I'm glad you saw them take him too. I thought I was going crazy or something." She uneasily tucks hair behind an ear. "I saw them take him and I couldn't do anything to help him."

"You're not crazy. I couldn't help him either. I was locked in." Gin knows strange things are happening and she's very unsettled by the lack of explanations and drugged state she's always kept in.

Marie looks back at her from the doorway. "I'm really glad you're here with me Gin. It's so nice to have someone normal to talk to around here for a change. Everyone around here is fucking useless. I'm not sure anyone else even knows what's going on in here." She looks down the hall before finishing, "We have to find Luke."

Gin nods. She has no idea how she could possibly find Luke,

but she knows that they need to try. Maybe they'll find a way out of here while they're exploring.

Marie runs from the room, her sneakers squeaking on the floor. Gin wraps her arms around her shoulders and rocks herself slightly. She can't really be stuck here.

A horrifying thought crosses her mind as the color washes from her face. If someone took Luke, what's stopping them from taking her or anyone else? Marie said that he wasn't the first. Oh shit. How can she get out? She knows she has got to try to get out.

She lays down and covers her head with the covers. She breathes her hot breath as she tries not to panic. She lays listening to the pipes and sounds around her, never removing the covers.

Later that night, Gin wakes up at the humming of the light overhead. She shields her eyes from the blinding light and sits up, waiting for someone to enter. Likely to give her more drugs, she thinks.

She looks around her room. Her window curtains are open. She doesn't remember opening them. She would have remembered opening them because she hates the view of the wall. It's dark outside the window and the brick wall isn't visible. She can't tell what time it is.

She stands up and stretches her neck to one side then the other. She walks to the window and reaches up to close the curtains. The lights flicker, leaving her, for a moment, in darkness. "That's odd." she says aloud. She looks out the window and strains to see something beyond the wall in any direction. There doesn't even seem to be moonlight.

The overhead lights flicker twice then stay on, making her try to adjust her sleepy eyes. She yawns and stretches some more, closing the dreary cream colored curtains to her window. From behind her she hears a soft voice call her name. She twists around thinking that a nurse had come in. There is no one there.

She stares in the direction she thought she'd heard it come from and quietly asks, "Is… is someone there?" She slowly steps toward the door. She tries to open the green metal door. Locked. She looks through the little window on the top, peering to one side then the other. A faint light is coming from somewhere down the hall, lighting the floor. No one was there though.

As if right behind her, she hears the raspy whisper of the voice, "You shouldn't be here Gin!" Gin freezes as the hairs on the back of her neck stand up. She slowly turns around to see only her desk and the bed behind her.

She drops to her knees calling out in an uncertain, shocked voice, "What do you want from me?" She bites her lower lip and tries not to show how scared she feels.

From the closet she hears, "They are going to take you away. You can't let them take you away."

She puts her hands over her ears, "No…No…No! Stop it!"

She shakes her head and closes her eyes hoping it will go away.

The rough voice, now seemingly coming from the closed window, says, "He's coming to take you away. He's going to kill you." She stands up and whips her head around trying to find the source of the voice.

She walks to her bed and hits the pillow with her closed fist. "Stop it. Stop it!"

Now the disembodied voice calls out to her from the directions of the door, "You can't trust them. They're trying to kill you. I can help you Gin."

She whips her hair as she runs to the door, pounding on its hard surface, almost hurting her hand. "Get me out of here! Someone help. Please help!" She looks out the tiny window as she pleads for anyone to hear her. There was only the light in the distance and the empty hallway.

As if whispered into her ear, "They won't help you. They will only hurt you with their medications. I can help you. I CAN help you."

Gins eyes widen as she slowly turns around. She was alone. The lights flicker several times making her heart race faster. Her palms are sweaty and she is breathing quickly and loudly through her mouth. She looks franticly around the room. No one is in the room with her.

Her nose feels wet and she feels like it is running down her face. She wipes it with the back of her hand. Blood. She wipes it again and her hand was soaked in crimson blood. She lets her face lean forward so it doesn't drain into her stomach and make her puke. She watches as blood drips from her face into a small puddle on the floor at her feet.

Again she hears the voice, this time from the other side of the room. "Gin you must be faster than him. You must NOT let him hurt you. He's going to take you away!"

Gin grabs a dirty black shirt off the floor and holds it up to her face to catch the flow of the metallic tasting fluid that is now lightly dripping from her face. She looks around from side to side. "Why are you doing this?"

A reply comes from the direction of the door and seems to echo in her head, "I want to help you Gin. I won't let them take you away. You have to listen to me. You can't let him kill you. He's coming!"

The overhead light flickers three more times, then dimly illuminates the room in a sickly blue with a humming of the light. Gin makes her way to the bed and sits on it, making the metal springs creak. She holds the shirt to her face and in a muffled voice says, "Why would they want to hurt me? I don't understand?!? They've already trapped me here. If they wanted to kill me why would they go through all this trouble?"

A deep cackle of a laugh fills the room, bouncing off the walls in several directions, "They are keeping you here. They know you shouldn't be here, but won't let you go till you're dead. You're so much smarter than them. They will hurt you to keep you here against your will. Don't let them Gin."

She sits up straighter in disbelief as the scratchy voice that was beginning to sound more masculine continues, "I will help you. He's going to bring medicine that will make you feel worse than you did earlier. They are giving you too much and this will be your final dose. They intend to make you go away for good."

Gin shakes her head. "That can't be." Her eyes swell up and she breaks out in a cold sweat. She can't, won't believe what she is hearing. She did feel like she was stuck, being held here against her will in this prison like cell, but there had to be another way to get out. She didn't want to get hurt, but didn't want to believe what she was hearing.

The light flickers once more, then stays on. Gin starts to hyperventilate. She wipes the sweat from her brow as she tastes metal in the back of her throat. The old concrete walls are closing in on her, but she can hardly see them. Her moist nose continues to drip into the shirt.

After a few minutes, she starts to feel like she can control her breathing and the room stops spinning. She notes that the taste in her mouth wasn't as nasty as it has been. She probably had a panic attack, she thought. A horrendous panic attack.

The heavy door makes a click-clock sound of being unlocked from the other side. Nurse Dale opens the door and peeks inside. "Gin are you awake?"

Cautiously Gin answers, "Yea, I'm up." He opens the door the rest of the way and she can see a cart behind him, probably full of medication. His blonde spikey hair and neatly tucked in shirt never move while he lets himself in the room.

He looks at her as though she has two heads. "You alright?"

Gin pulls the shirt away from her face to talk to him. It is dry. She holds her hands in front of her face. The blood was gone. Not a drop. She raises her head and answers, "I think so." She sits motionless on the edge of the bed for a moment with her face wrinkled up staring into the shirt in her hand.

A low raspy voice whispers, "Gin don't let him hurt you. He means to hurt you." She tries to shake the feeling that she is in danger.

Nurse Dale looks her over then starts digging in one side of the rolling metal cart with the locking doors. She hears metal clanking together and pill bottles rustling around. "Ah, there they are." He pours some pills into a white cup and sits something just out of her sight in the top of the cart with a loud clankety-clop. He walks over closer to her and holds out a cup of pills. "Here you go. These are for you." He has a strange look on his face and Gin is unsure if she should take them from him.

She takes the pills in her hand and looks at them closely. These are not the usual white and yellow ones that she'd been given before. These are blue caplets and larger yellow pills plus a half of a light green one. Gin shakes her head. "These aren't right. I've never seen these before."

Dale has a gleam in his eye as he says, almost too calmly, "The doctor has changed your prescriptions."

She tries to give them back, "No, I wasn't told of any changes. I'm not taking these until the Doc tells me they've been changed."

Dale's face grows angry. "You WILL take your meds little girl.

I don't want to have to force them down your throat, but I will."

Gin pulls her hand full of pills back and looks at him in horror. "I don't want to take them."

The voice whispers in her ear, "Gin don't take the pills! He's going to try to hurt you."

Dale gets closer to her and in a nasty tone of voice says, "You have to take them. I will make you if you wanna do this the hard way."

Gin feels a shiver run down her whole body. She tries hard not to show him that he can intimidate her. But he did, in fact, scare her.

From behind the nurse the voice calls to her. "He has a syringe on the cart! He's going to restrain you if you let him. The straps are in his back pocket." Gin freezes as she figures out what to do. "He's going to take your unconscious body away on the cart. That's why he brought it."

Nurse Dale looks at her, wild-eyed, as she puts the pills in her mouth and takes the water to wash them down. "Now open up." He demands of her in a deep, fierce tone. He leans in to check the contents of her mouth.

Gin takes a breath and spits the pills and water as hard as she can in his face. He turns and wipes his face in his hands, yelling, "You dumb bitch!"

Gin sees the restraints in his back pocket and darts to the cart. He catches her wrist as she runs, nearly knocking her down. He reaches for a strap in his pocket with his free hand while she twists and contorts her body trying to free herself from his constricted grasp. She drops to the ground and kicks at him as hard as she can while yelling, "Noooo. Leave me alone! I won't take them!" Laying on her back she kicks a second time, this time striking him square in the jaw.

He releases her as he howls in pain, hunkered over, grabbing his chin. "You stupid bitch. I can't believe you did that."

Gin scrambles to get the cart in between him and herself. There is a syringe sitting on the top. She grabs it, puts it in her pocket, and kicks the cart as hard as she can, hitting him in the head while bent over. An assortment of pills come spilling out the front of the cabinet all over the floor around her feet. Dale screeches in pain and Gin grimaces and looks away as the cart strikes him.

Dale falls to the ground while yelling, "I'm going to get you, you stupid fucking bitch! Get back here. Damn it!"

From behind her the hoarse voice shrieks, "Don't let him hurt you. Do it now." Gin slams the cart into him a second time making him fall to the floor. He scrambles to get up as she rams it into him a third time, knocking him down completely. The metal cart clanks and bangs, echoing around the room.

He continues to scream at her and tries to get to his knees as she kicks the hard metal cart again, this time hitting him in the head as he charges toward her like a bull. He howls in pain as the cart runs over his hand and smashes into his face.

Again she kicks with all her might, pushing him to the wall. She knows he was going to hurt her. She is positive of it. She shoves the cart hard once more and hears a loud crack as his head is sandwiched between the cart and the concrete wall. Blood gushes from Dale's head, but he still reaches for her with his mangled, run over hand.

Gin knows she has to push harder than she has ever pushed before and rams the cart into him again as hard and as fast as she can. She pushes the cart over onto him, the remaining pills scurry around the room and fall into the blood that has pooled around him. She stops when she sees him stop moving, stop coming for her.

She bends over and tries to catch her breath. Blood splatter covers the wall behind Dale's body under the cart. It begins to drip down the already stained walls. Gin yells out in disgust as she pulls the cart from his mutilated body and watches to see if he moves.

His face has been completely smashed, and resembles a smashed pumpkin, pieces from the inside hanging out. His teeth have gone through his lips and his tongue hangs, blood dripping down it like a faucet. He no longer resembles a person at all. She kicks at him and when she is convinced that he is actually probably dead and not going to come at her again, she searches his pockets for keys. They must be here somewhere she thinks.

Gin dry heaves at the sight of his face and his caved in nose. She didn't want to look at the grotesque man in front of her. She throws up beside him as his open wounds drip blood all over her hands and arms as she tries desperately to find the keys. She finds them in the second side pocket she goes through and quickly yanks them from the attached key ring on his pants. She tries to turn her head away.

The coarse voice seems to be in front of her now. "Run Gin. Just run." She unhooks the keys from the ring as she fights back the urge to vomit, which is stinging the back of her throat. She heaves as she grasps the keys tight in her hand as blood drips between her fingers.

She scrambles to her feet, slipping on the now immense pool of blood around her. "Auuugh!" She screams as she quickly gains her balance and lunges toward the door, gripping it and banging it open as she hurriedly tries to leave the room. Her bare feet squeak on the slippery floor as she runs down the hallway, trying hard not to lose her balance.

She runs to Marie's room and tries to unlock the door. Marie sleepily looks back at her through the little opening. Yelling echoes through the hall as Marie motions for her to go. Her lips mouth 'run' through the glass window. Gin turns and runs. Her lungs burn as she makes her way down the hall.

She peers over the stairs and sees no one, so she runs down the flight of stairs to the door underneath.

Behind her the voice encourages her. "You've almost got it now, Gin." She wipes her hands off on the underside of her shirt, removing the sticky drying liquid from her fingers. She fumbles with the keys to find the one that fits in the now locked door. The third silver key she tries fits and she turns the handle. In her panic she breaks the key off in the door lock as she hurries through it.

She gasps for breath as she runs down the hallway toward the double doors. She hears pounding on the door behind her and unintelligible yelling. She looks back over her shoulder as she runs.

A light flickers in the hall in front of her next to a door that is cracked open. She hears the lock on the door start to open behind her and hurries into the opened doorway, pulling it closed behind her. She flips the light switch off. She stands up against the wall trying to breathe quietly as she hears footsteps run past her outside in the hall. She is covered in sweat and puts her hands on her knees and braces herself as she tries to breathe. She wipes her brow with her shirt collar as she tries to slow her breathing to listen.

She hears yelling at the end of the hallway, then more running footsteps and muffled yelling in the other direction, toward the double doors. She stands there until she can't hear them anymore then she waits longer. She grips the doorknob, takes a deep breath and cracks the door open enough to look down the hall. The lights flicker in the hall above her. She puts her head out and looks around before opening the door and running toward the double doors further down the hallway. She fumbles to find the right key, drops the keys. She quickly retrieves them and continues to try to find the right key. "Where is it?!?"

Finally she finds a perfect fit and pushes the bar, opening one of the doors. She peaks out of the door and, seeing the coast is clear, runs for the end of the hallway. There must be a way out of here.

The door just before the end of the hall reads 'stairs'. She grabs the handle and finds it unlocked so she yanks it open and runs as fast as she can down the first flight of stairs. Then the next. She holds onto the railing for support as she races down three floors of concrete and metal stairs.

As she runs down the next flight of stairs, she hears a door next to her being opened from the other side. She gasps and races down the stairs, tripping twice and catching herself on the metal railing. She comes to the bottom of the stairs and hears yelling and footsteps above her in the stairwell. The door is locked.

Gin tries desperately to find a key for the door. Finally, heart racing, she slides the correct key into the lock and turns the handle as the footsteps get closer. She pulls the door closed behind her to finds she is in another hallway with double doors ahead.

She scrambles to reach the far doors on other side as she hears yelling and keys at the door behind her. She drops the keys again as she searches to find the one for the door. As she reaches down to grab them, the door opens and Steve steps through in front of her. Her jaw drops as she is met face-to-face with Steve.

He grips her hair with a tattooed hand as she turns to run, yanking her backwards and sending a shooting pain through her head. She screams in pain as she jets back toward him like a rubber band.

Steve holds her tight by the hair as he yells over his shoulder, "Found her." He loosens his grip as he holds her by both arms facing away from him. He tries to stay calm as he says, "You can't get out of here. I hoped you'd play nice and follow the rules. Here you are, out of your room."

Gin tries to free herself as she yells, "Nooo. Let me go!" She thrashes to try to free herself from him. He pushes her up against the wall as he is joined by more orderlies and security guards. "You can't do this. Let me go!"

Steve's voice is stern as he orders, "Sedate her already." Gin kicks him in the shins and tries one last time to get away, but she isn't strong enough.

She feels her sleeve move and the sting of a needle in her shoulder. She tries to fight, pinned to the wall. The room starts to spin as her eyes get heavy. She tries to yell but her tongue feels swollen and she coughs instead. She shakes her head as if it would stop anything. She strains to turn her head and sees two of the doors. She feels herself go limp as she can no longer struggle. She feels her body being lifted. Her eyes close as sounds swirl together and everything goes black.

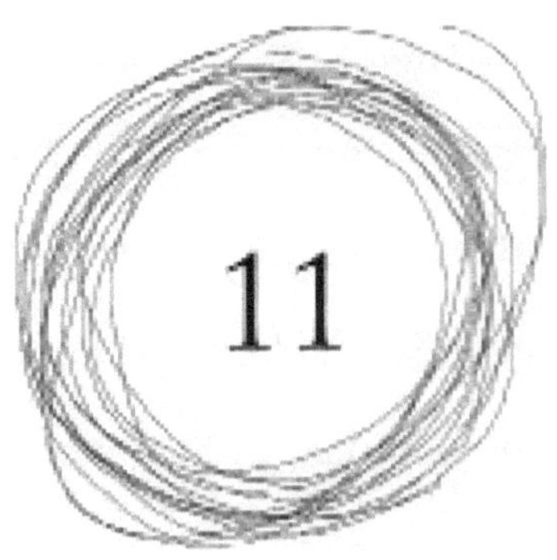

11

Gin's eyes sting. She rubs them as she tries to shake the feeling of going right back to sleep. She fights to stay awake. She's cold and grasps the covers around her neck as she strains to open her sleepy eyes. The light from the hallway does little to comfort her.

She lies still for several minutes as vivid pictures play in her head from the night before. She pulls her hand to her face to look at it in the dimly lit room. Her hand is clean. The light flickers on.

Gin slings her feet over the side of the bed and sits up, rubbing her eyes and yawning. The room is clean. She rubs a sore spot on her shoulder. She could feel where they stabbed her with a needle. She hadn't possibly dreamed that. Had they moved her to another craptacular room? Nothing seemed out of place. The same nasty stains that she has studied for hours in her boredom are in the same place they were before. The disgusting desk still sits in the corner with the box sitting on it.

If this is the same room, where is all the blood? There's no way it could all have been cleaned? Is there? She did get drugged. She could have been out for days, for all she knows. She cringes at the thought of them being good at cleaning blood. That would mean they might do it often enough to be good at it.

Gin hears shuffling on the other side of the door. She pulls her feet up and hugs her knees as she faces the door, not sure what will be there.

Nurse Bettie clears her throat as she enters the room. "I see you got yourself up." She pulls a squeaky cart behind her. A slender, darker man follows the Nurse into the room. "This is Ron Jon, he'll be helping us out around here." She looks into Gin's eyes. "I trust you won't cause him problems."

Gin shakes her head no. She sits quietly as Bettie unlocks and retrieves a bottle from the cart. Gin looks Ron Jon over, unsure of his warm grin. He speaks up, "Hi Gin, I'll be taking you to group today, if you're feeling better." His voice seems soft, yet outspoken.

Nurse Bettie holds a pill in front of Gin in a paper cup. "Take this." She offers her another water cup. Gin takes the pill and swallows it with a swish. She does not have the energy to fight right now and she knows she'll be sleeping again soon. They don't let her stay awake long. "Open", Bettie demands. Gin opens her mouth and resist sticking her tongue out at her. "Thank you Gin."

With a loud slam and then a clump, the cart is once again locked tight. It startles Gin, even though she expects it. She rubs her groggy eyes again with the palm of her hand. She looks over the top of her hand again. She is completely clean of blood. That gritty soap in the showers could scrub your skin off. She decides not to ask about her hands or the room. She may be slapped by Nurse Bettie. She can tell she's pretty mad at her.

Nurse Bettie steps closer to Gin. Her expression turns sterner than normal. Gin gulps hard and opens her eyes wider. Bettie's voice is firm as she says, "I expect you to show Ron Jon respect. I don't have to let you out of here today. Not after the crap you pulled last night. I should leave you in this room to think about it." She straightens and continues, "I'm a reasonable person, but you are going to have to fol-low the rules better if you want to heal."

Gin cringes, trying not to be visible. She knows how they're 'healing' her. They're keeping her captive and subjecting her to abuse. She has a strong feeling some of the others are being treated worse. She doesn't want to know what they are capable of and she's very weak at the moment.

Ron Jon says, "We'll get along great. Isn't that right Gin?" Gin nods. He places a banana on her desk, then returns to his position at the door. Completely agreeing is just easier right now. She knows she wouldn't have a chance of winning any sort of reasonable argument. Certainly not with the two of them there.

Gin pushes out a soft, "Yea." She looks past Bettie at the guy with well-groomed dark hair. His hands are neatly clasped and his head is cocked to one side. His smile seems genuine. Kill 'em with kindness, she thinks as she watches them filter back out into the hallway.

"I'll see you for lunch." Ron Jon adds as he pulls the door closed behind them.

Gin blinks long and hard a couple of times. She lays back down with a huge sigh. A soft groan escapes her lips as she covers herself back up. For now she is happy to have a bed and to be alone. Pulling the blankets over her head, she is able to block out the light piercing her eyes from above.

She lies trying not to think about anything. She stares at the blanket and takes slow breaths to slow her heart. She doesn't know what will happen, but she knows that she's tired. She closes her eyes and welcomes sleep. Sleep can take it all away, even if for just a little while.

12

Marie sits on her bed as Gin walks by her room. She must have been done with the doctors, she wasn't around earlier when Gin had looked for her. Marie's head is resting on one knee, pulled up close to her body. She leans on the dingy brick wall. She looks up through a sea of dark brown hair when she realizes Gin is standing in the doorway. She pushes some of the locks out of her eyes and opens her lips to speak, but nothing comes out. Warm tears stain her face.

"What did they do to you?" Gin's face wrinkles up.

Marie pulls her other leg up to her chest and locks her hands tight around them, burying her face in her knees. She slowly rocks herself and sobs. After a moment she raises her face and Gin can see her swollen red eyes and red puffy cheeks, drenched in salty tears. "Dr. Veinkman made me talk about it. How I FEEL about it. I..I.. don't want to anymore, I want to move on. He says that talking about feelings will help me heal. Do I look fucking healed to you?!?" She balls her fists and twists up her face.

Gin sits next to her on the bed a few feet away. Marie hits the bed with her fists in frustration several times while sobbing and sniffling. Marie wipes her runny nose on the back of her hand then looks directly at Gin. "How can I heal, if I can't be allowed to move on?!"

"How long have you been here?"

"Too l ..long." She sobs. "Seems like all I can remember anymore."

"Even as a kid?" Gin asked, urging her to share even an ounce more about her dark past.

"That's when it happened." She pulls her face into her knees again and Gin can hear her crying through her snotty tears. Marie turns her face back toward Gin, leaving it on her lap. Tears streams down the side of her nose and drip onto her jeans. In a hushed voice she says," We were all just kids. They were my friends. There were four of us: Caroline, Mike, Ken, and me. We grew up together. Caroline was my best friend."

She sits up and wipes more tears with the back of her hands. She takes a deep breath while looking at the ceiling and continues, "We were the trouble makers I guess. It was mainly the guys, but we had fun pulling pranks too. Mike and Caroline had been pretty close for a few years, he was really sweet to her and she was sure he was going to help her get out of this shit ass town someday. She was going to be an actress…" Her voice trails.

She takes another deep breath then another. She buries her face again and continues to sob and then tries to catch her breath as tears flow freely from her soaked face. She throws her hair back and, still squeakily crying, tries to calm herself down wiping more salty tears with her sleeves.

"You can tell me what happened Marie."

She sniffles several times and states, "As we got older the guys started pulling some pretty awful stuff; burning abandoned farmhouses, bullying street people, looting, stealing, anything they could do and get away with really. Ken was usually the one with the grand ideas; he despised being a preacher's son. Caroline was the most creative though." For a second Marie half smiles then continues to sob. Her face soaked in tears; she pounds her fists twice on the bed again making the whole thing shake.

"One day all four of us were hanging out in the field by the old mall on the couches we had put there years ago. Our fire was burning in the pit to fight the crisp cold morning air. Ken was upset because we hadn't been doing anything that he considered mischievous enough. He accused Mike of just wanting to spend his time taking Caroline to the movies and not wanting to do things like they used to do. The guys made a plan to break into a pawn shop in the following days. It was a really simple plan; the owner was really predictable and had fake cameras in his shop. They would just go in armed with a bat and a machete; loot the place and get out really fast." She trails off again.

Marie takes a deep breath and continues, "The night of the break-in, there was a fire that burned down the pawn shop and the apartments above. Burnt to the ground. Mike never made it out."

Gin stares at her wide-eyed, listening intently as she continues, "Caroline and I were at her parents' house doing homework at the kitchen table when Ken came to tell us what had happened. We were studying, but also talking about how we could fill some of the balloons, at our up-and-coming dance, with shaving foam as a joke. We always joked about how to embarrass the snotty kids we went to school with. We wanted to mess up those expensive dresses they bought that neither Caroline nor I could afford."

Marie went quiet for a moment. "Ken stormed in and we could tell something was wrong right away. He told us about the fire. He said Mike didn't come out after him. He was supposed to be right behind him… He kept looking out the window to see if he had been followed."

"Caroline couldn't control her hysteria. She just kept yelling at Ken that it was his fault that Mike hadn't come back. She screamed that Ken should have made sure his best friend was right behind him. How could he do this to Mike? Or to her? Mike couldn't be dead. He just couldn't be!"

Marie looks at the floor and sniffles a glob of snot inside her nose. She has trouble controlling her voice. "He told us we couldn't go to the police that we would all go to jail."

Marie stopped, repositioned her uncomfortable position and tried to steady her voice. "Caroline was out of control screaming at him. She just kept saying how could you do this to him, he was your best friend? I was shocked at the news, I had just seen him earlier in the day when he had picked me up to go to Caroline's. He had brought me to where I was; Caroline too. I remember trying to ask what happened, but Ken just kept saying, 'It wasn't supposed to be like this, Goddamn it, not like this.'"

"What did you do?" Gin asks quietly.

"I tried to make sense of it in my mind; we had just lost our good friend, for unexplained reasons. Caroline became more hysterical and Ken yelled at her to stop and be quiet so he could think which made her cry harder. She yelled that she didn't want anything to do with any of this, she just wanted Mike. Ken told her to shut up so he could think, Mike was dead."

Marie wipes her nose again and sobs fill her lungs. The bed squeaks as she rocks herself gently to calm down. After a few minutes she continues, "I watched in shock as he ripped her up from the table by the wrist and pushed her up against the flocked wallpaper of the kitchen next to the fridge of her parents' house. He started yelling in her face that she needed to shut her stupid fucking face while he figures out what to do."

Marie licks her lips and tucks hair behind her ear while deep in thought. "I snapped at him to leave her alone, she didn't do anything. He grabbed a canary yellow ceramic canister off the counter and threw it at me. It grazed my head before smashing into jagged shards on the tile floor." Marie motions past her temple with her hand and then rubs a spot on the side of her head; feeling with her fingertips. "Caroline struggled to free herself from him, twisting and turning, ripping her shirt from the grasp he had on her shoulder. He pinned her to the wall and she wanted him to let go. He yelled to stop as she kicked and spit at him. He went into a rage and threw her to the floor so hard that she hit her head. I watched in terror as she laid there unmoving." Marie starts to cry again.

Gin waits patiently, unsure and uncomfortable. She finds

herself squirming as her stomach leaps to her throat as Marie remembers her past. She watches as Marie covers her face with her hands and shakes her head.

"Ken turned to me with a gleam in his eyes I'd never seen before. All I remember is him saying over and over again that we had to just calm down and that everything would be fine. I screamed at him that Caroline was hurt and I had to get her to the doctor. I had to help her!" She shakes her head violently as the memories pour in. "He told me that we weren't going anywhere. I had backed further and further toward Caroline's living room, he was much faster and stronger than I was. I looked at Caroline on the kitchen floor, bleeding from the head, and saw her eyes open for a split second. I wanted to help her. I needed to help my best friend! I could smell Ken's hot breath in my face as he grabbed my wrists and ranted about how no one could find out and anyone in his way would have to be kept quiet." She takes another long deep breath. She rocks herself for a minute as Gin feels as though she is watching the frail looking girl unravel at the seams.

"I told him that he couldn't do this as he slapped me repeatedly, making my face burn red. I felt my head hit what I can only guess was the banister in the living room, and the walls started spinning. I saw Caroline, face and hair covered in her own blood, lunge

at Ken with a huge kitchen knife. It caught him in the shoulder making him let go of me and spin around toward her. I fell as he wrestled
Caroline for the knife and pried it from her fingers as she screamed
at him. I was trying to stand. I couldn't get my balance as Ken took
the knife from her and stabbed her violently, over and over again."

Marie gasps in-between sobs, laying her head in her knees to muffle the sounds of her heartache. Gin wants to hug her, do anything to help her feel better. All she can do is utter, "Oh my god."

"I know!" Marie yell-whispers toward the ceiling. She tries desperately to calm herself, wiping steaming tears from her neck and face before continuing. "She rolled over and tried to crawl away... He...He kept stabbing her even after she stopped screaming. I could hear him grunt as the knife made a thud sound in her."

Gin felt her stomach roll as Marie spoke and she felt like she could hear it too. Every scream. She knew Marie remembers vividly what happened to her childhood friend and can't imagine how she feels. She finds herself crying quietly next to Marie on the bed.

"I could reach a large piece of the canister that he threw at me. It had broken all over the floor. It cut my hand as I gripped it. I jumped at Ken and stabbed him in the back of the neck. He turned toward me and I stabbed him again in the eye, with all my might."

Marie motioned with her hand in a tight fist as she stared at the scene unfolding somewhere beyond the wall in front of her. She was in a daze as her face twisted and she stabbed at the air. She held her breath for a second and sniffled.

"He yelled in pain as the shard stuck out from his face spraying blood all over me. I scrambled to find another weapon before he could come after me again. The only thing I saw was the knife sticking out of Caroline's back… I was crying…I…" Marie trailed for a second. "I pulled the knife out of her lifeless, blood soaked body. She… She made a gurgling sound as I yanked it out. I screamed as I pulled the knife from my best friend."

Gin covers her mouth with her hand at the thought. "Oh fuck. What did you do? Did he hurt you?!?"

Marie gets quiet. She stares at the wall in front of them, then looks at Gin with her wet, blood-shot eyes. Her lips turn up in a smirk. "If it weren't for Dr. Veinkman, I wouldn't remember any of it. I didn't until two years ago, ya know." She laughs a deep laugh that startles Gin a little. "He deserved what I had to do to him, I know that now." Marie stares into Gin's eyes, she can feel her gaze as she continued," I cut his throat."

Gin bites her knuckle as Marie continues," I jumped at him

and wrapped my arm around, and pulled the knife as hard as I could. I watched him reach and scratch as if there was anything he could do as blood poured from his throat. He fell into a pool of his own blood on the tile just where he belonged. Fucking prick."

"That's how you ended up here? For defending yourself?"

"No. No there's more. Shhhh." She puts her finger to her lips to hush and quickly wipes her eyes.

Nurse Bettie appears in her matching Tibetan pant suit, hair neat and tidy, just like her desk and routine. She looks at them inquisitively, then sighs. "You need to be in group in ten minutes. Only reminder. Got it?"

"Got it," they both reply coldly.

"Awe Gin are you having a rough day?"

"No I'm fine."

"Well let's make sure we keep ourselves under control. We can't have you losing it in group now can we." Nurse Bettie looks at her sternly.

"Really, I'm fine." She assures her, trying to get her to go without dragging her off with her. She clearly wasn't okay right now. Marie clearly wasn't alright either. She didn't need to be sedated though.

"I won't disrupt group Bettie."

Nurse Bettie raises an eyebrow and looks both girls up and down. "Be in group in ten minutes." She turns and walks down the hallway.

Gin looks at Marie who was still looking at the doorway, staring rather. "ARE you okay?" she asks, knowing the answer already.

"I'm never okay. I've learned to live with it, with all these thoughts swimming in my mind." She shifts her gaze back to Gin. "We don't have long."

"I know, if we're late for group we'll be in deep shit…"

Marie cuts her off, "No WE don't have long. We need to get out of here before it's too late. I know you've heard them too. They told me."

"What?! What do you mean? The voice?"

"Of course I mean the goddamn voices. They won't stop until you listen."

"I've found speakers in the rooms… and wires, which must be where they're coming from. I'm still working on figuring it out, but there must be an explanation for voices in here. I've seen speakers throughout the whole damned building…They're probably try-

133

ing to freak me out."

"Sure, the explanation is that it's all in your head. They burrowed their way in and are nesting now. You won't find an explanation, believe me, I've tried. It knows things that no one should know." She shook her head, "They make you listen."

Gin straightens out her shoulders and narrows her eyes. She knows they have to get to group and she's a freaking mess right now. "How did you get here?" She really needs to know.

Marie falls silent again, but her gaze never wavers from Gin. She doesn't blink. "After I killed Ken… I went home."

Gin is starting to get a bit uncomfortable as Marie stares straight through her. Even though she can tell Marie isn't actually looking at her anymore, Gin squirms a little on the bed next to her. She crosses and uncrosses her legs as Marie goes on, "I walked the five miles from Caroline's house to mine, still holding the knife I had used to kill Ken. The knife he used to kill Caroline. No one noticed me or asked if I needed help. I felt invisible. When I got home I took a shower. I scrubbed his blood from my arms and face and watched as it swirled dark chunks and pink down the drain at my feet, surrounding my toes. I went to my room, started to get dressed in clean clothes, and I could hear someone come home. The front door slammed downstairs. I could hear banging around in the hall-way and I knew that my dad was drunk again. I opened the door and walked down the grimy, carpeted hallway toward the stairs."

Marie falls silent again and looks at the floor. She pulls the bottom of her shirt down and straightens her jeans a bit nervously. "I had to."

"Had to what?" Gin asks.

"I had to make him stop hurting my mom."

13

Gin looks out the window through the gray rain. It's pouring down the glass, pooling from small streams into rivers. She almost makes out the garden several floors below, seemingly sprinkled in little lights. George tried to tell her about the courtyard and garden and how she'd like it when she was allowed. She wasn't sure when he had told her, yesterday maybe. His giggling was more than she could take and she had politely walked away from the conversation entirely. Tonight though, the shadows of the night were lit up. She looks for hope in the shadows.

Behind her, patients babble and watch television. She doesn't give a shit about any of them right now. She rubs her wrist and remembers how she'd woken up restrained in bed and Ron Jon explaining he'd like to let her up, but it was doctor's orders till she calmed down. She makes a fist and rolls her wrist around, shuddering for a second as she bends her wrists back.

She is a little annoyed when Alfred abandons his post at another window to talk to her. "You sure look chipper this afternoon my dear." He has his usual genuine suave tone.

She doesn't look at him as she sarcastically replies, "I'm the happiest I've ever been."

Alfred clutches his heart. "If only I was thirty years younger, I'd sweep you off your feet to a reasonably beautiful life." He sighs and shakes his head.

Gin puts her fingertips on the cold glass as she looks blankly out the window. Pretending that he hadn't just spoken she wonders aloud, "I wonder if I'll ever see outside these walls again."

Alfred scratches his head. "They say the way out is to get healed. I believe that is true. You'll be out there... *Banana gram*!! running to wherever your heart leads you."

She sighs deeply and looks at Alfred. "I don't understand why I'm here at all."

He motions to sit on a nearby couch and sits on one side. "I didn't always want to be in business. I realize it's shocking, but it's true. When I was a boy, I wanted nothing more than to be a veterinarian. That was of course, before I found out about those hearty wormy-bugs and fleas. Did you know pets have fleas!?" He visibly shudders. "So disgusting to think that you're harboring a bug host."

Gin gives a half smile. She sets on the sofa with him, crossing her legs. She leans away from him as they sit. Curious she asks, "You never had a pet because you were scared of bugs?" A little laugh follows her question.

"No, well… my ex-wife had a cat that licked itself! It licked its own paws. She said that they liked to stay clean. The places that cat licked! Then!" His index finger points up. "Then it would assume I was an IMBECILE and would try to come get my affections with that same nasty mouth."

Quickly, half-switching subjects, Alfred adds plainly, "Everything happens for a reason, even if we don't quite know why ourselves. The universe is so vast and powerful in its magnificence-ness, there's no way we could predict our own lives." Gin wiggles, around in her seat becoming uninterested.

He sits up straighter and continues, "Look at it this way. Before my accident, I was married to a disaster of a woman, but wasn't able to see it until I got my little scratch here." He points to the giant bald spot on the side of his head. Gin raises her eyebrows as he speaks. "I couldn't have foreseen it coming, but it did come. The truth about the world was revealed in a hospital room while she spouted all the reasons why she felt she should have left me years ago, Banana gram!... mostly it was her dark lover Fernando." Gins eyes widen and she makes herself not react or smirk.

He clears his throat, covering his mouth politely. "Sure, I had a serious head wound and was in traction, but that moment set in motion a series of events that were already set in motion with a pipe iron to the head." He smiles. "Every day is worthy of living, even here in the most unlikely of places. You should try to enjoy life."

"Pipe Iron, huh?" Gin shudders. "Sorry to hear your ex-wife is more of a bitch than I'd thought. While in traction? Really? Wow." He nods his head and crosses his arms.

Gin pats him on the shoulder quickly. "You're a good guy. I have to find out why I'm here and why I haven't heard from my friends. No visits or calls. I don't think they know I'm here like the Doc says."

She looks around and behind her shoulder to see if Marie has shown up in the common room yet. She hasn't seen her all day and it would be a great reason to slip away from Alfred and his nonsensical chatter.

Alfred inquires, "Not even a letter or a telephone call?! There must be something? That doesn't at all sound like family."

Gin shakes her head, "I haven't been able to contact anyone and they just say that it's all taken care of. Joe would call me if he could. If he had any idea of where I was, I'd have heard from him by now. I'm positive he would help me." She was growing frustrated and didn't feel better about her situation. Her nose wrinkled up and she sighed.

Alfred places his hand on the tip of his scraggly chin while he ponders for a second. "You'll have the answers soon, I'm sure of it. This is a good place. There are much worse places to be." He stands up and gives a bow, holding one arm out. "I must retire to contemplate. Goodbye Gin."

She waves as he swiftly gets up and goes back to the other window. "Bye."

14

"Wake up Gin. They're coming." Gin wakes abruptly. She distinctly hears the voice that had awoken her. She rubs her eyes and looks around the nearly barren room trying to find the source. She is alone. "You have to get up now!" The raspy voice insists from across the room. She strains her eyes to peer through the darkness at the source, but there's nothing there. She doesn't know what time it is, but the lights were still off in her room. The door seems locked. "You have to get up now." The deep voice repeats, prompting Gin to sit up in her squeaky bed.

She pushes hair behind her ear and looks around. "Who's there?" She asks in a hushed tone into the darkness. There is no reply, but she is certain she'd heard it. She pulls the scratchy white blankets back and starts to get up, trying to orient herself with her surroundings after having been in a deep, medication induced sleep. "Is someone there?" Again, no answer.

Seeming to come from the closet this time, the voice grows

more impatient, "Get up Gin. Get up now. They're coming." She looks in the direction the voice is coming from and can see the outline of the dark, empty closet. No one is there in the shadows.

She stands up and walks in the dark to the closet, examining it. Her clothes are stacked on the attached shelf above her head, but certainly no one is in it. She squints to see across the room through the blackness. "Who's there?" she asks, again reaching her arms out toward the source of the voice. She thinks there must be some sort of speaker or something that the voice is coming from. She runs her fingertips over the coarse concrete wall searching for the source of the voice. There is nothing there.

"Gin you're in danger here. They're coming now." This time the sound of the scratchy voice comes from somewhere by the heavy metal door behind her. Startled, she jumps then whips her head around in the direction it came from. "You are in danger."

Gin feels a chill creep up her spine as she looks in the direction of the voice. "What?" She makes her way through the dark to the heavy metal door, pushing and pulling on it. It was definitely locked.

She feels around, searching desperately to find the speaker the voice is coming from. There must be someone playing a trick on her. She tries to find a wire or something around the door as she feels around the cold door frame in the dark, digging her bitten nails around the edges to find something to grab. Nothing there. "Who's there?" Gin yells out into the darkness that engulfs her.

The light above her head flickers a sickly blue and washes the soiled walls with light. For a moment, she can tell there is no one else in the space with her. Then it's washed in black again.

She looks around franticly for the source of the voice. Again the lights flicker on then off a few times. Complete darkness surrounds her. Gin pulls her arms in and puts her hands over her ears and squeezes her eyes shut as she yells, "Leave me alone!"

She looks around in the dark, feeling the musty air enclose her as she makes her way back to the bed. She tucks her head into her legs that she has pulled tightly to her body and takes a deep breath to calm down. She lets out another sigh and wonders if someone is pulling a trick on her.

A low pitched whisper by her ear makes her gasp aloud. "He's going to take you away for good."

"Stop it! Stop it! Just stop it!" She yells as she covers her ears, shaking her head on her lap. "Leave me alone!"

A raspy reply comes from the doorway. "You can't let him hurt you." The sound makes her skin crawl as the disembodied voice continues, "You'll have to think fast this time. He's going to drug you again. That's when he'll do it." The low hiss echoes through her ears, "You're not safe anymore."

Gin looks toward the door, shaking her head. "No! Stop it! Stop doing this." Her voice trails as she pleads in her own head for the horrible hoax to end. Her bottom lip quivers as she tries to gain the courage to continue shouting at the nothingness in the dark. "You're wrong."

The moving voice teases from the corner beside her, "You're going to have to act fast. He's going to come in alone and he's going to have a syringe and a knife in his pocket. If you don't act, he'll take you away for good. I know what he's planning. I want to help you."

She starts breathing heavily, feeling pressure on her heart as sweat begins to bead up on her forehead. She looks, wild-eyed, into the darkness. "Why won't you stop?"

Seeming to come from the door again, the mysterious voice becomes raspier, like being forced through a squeaking door hinge. "I just want you to be safe Gin. They mean to harm you. They all do. He's coming, but you can stop him from taking you upstairs."

In disbelief she shakes her head again. "No one's taking me upstairs. I haven't done anything wrong." As soon as she finishes her words the lights flicker again, making her gasp and hold a hand to her mouth to stop her from yelling out.

Quietly the voice laughs a deep, cackling, laugh that echoes around the room. "You're here against your will. They won't stop until you're dead." Laughter fills the room as the lights flicker and flutter once again in their bluish hue. "Upstairs is where the old-fashioned treatment facility is and the morgue, dear girl."

She wraps her arms tightly around herself for comfort as she holds in a sob. "No, that's not true. Maximum security is upstairs."

She jumps as the voice barks, "WRONG. He's going to drug you up and if you don't cooperate he's going to choke you. He's not afraid to use the knife. He's done it before. You have to think and act fast."

Breathing heavily Gin grimaces at the idea of spending another day so heavily medicated that she can barely hold open her eyelids. They want to slam shut now, on their own, in a cloud of haziness. She doesn't know where the voice is coming from, but what it has said can hardly be ignored. The light fixture flickers again, this time humming and crackling as though the light might burst. "Who are you?!" She stutters, trying not to let her voice squeak.

From a few feet away the raspy, coarse voice replies, "Think and act fast. He will be here anytime now. Don't let him get you." Gin's breathing remains heavy and quick as she stares into the darkness.

The heavy door makes a clink-clunk sound as it unlocks. Gin gasps and turns her attention to the door, not sure what to expect next. She quickly throws the covers over herself and lies down. She pretends to be asleep. The light turns on and she squeezes her eyes shut, her heart pounding so hard she thinks it will leap from her chest.

The door slowly creaks open and Nurse Bronson enters carrying several items: a cup of pills, a clipboard and pen. "Gin wake up. It's time for your nighttime meds." Gin shields her eyes from the bright light and pretends to have just woken up. She sits up and looks at him blankly. "Here are your meds," he says sternly, "and get that stupid look off you face before I smack it off."

She argues apprehensively, "I don't want them." His dark tanned face wrinkles up in disapproval. He had pushed the door so that it was barely cracked open.

Nurse Bronson turns to her and in a hushed voice says, "I had a feeling you were going to be trouble. You know I'm going to make you take them. If you can't follow the rules, you'll have to go upstairs." He reaches out and grabs her by the wrist squeezing hard. He reaches into his back pocket with his free hand.

From right beside Gin the voice whispers. "Do it now. Act now!" Bronson pulls a syringe full of clear yellowish liquid from behind him, his angry eyes gleaming at her. Gin kicks at him, trying to free herself from his grasp, knocking the pills, pen and the clipboard onto the floor with a loud clatter.

His grip tightens around her wrist as she wriggles to get loose and tries to back away from him. "Now you've done it." He pulls the cap off the syringe with his teeth as she kicks as hard as she can, hitting the elbow that held her captive. He yells out in pain as he loosens his grip just enough for her to scramble away. He grabs the back of her shirt, causing her to spin and fall to the hard concrete floor. The side of her face hits the ground with a smack that leaves her dizzy. "God dammed bitch! Now you're going to get it."

She tries to crawl away from him and hears her shirt rip slightly as she tries with all her might to get away from him. He yanks her back and she can see the gleam of the sharp needle. She kicks at him again, this time freeing herself and crawling on her knees toward the door. "No! Leave me alone!" She reaches out and grabs the pen from the floor, clenching it tightly.

The voice yells to her, "Do it now. NOW!" Without hesitation Gin grabs the pen as tightly as she can and rolls to face Bronson. He is coming at her like a mad bull with the sharp syringe in his hand.

She yells as she lunges at him and plunges the pen into his throat, right below his Adam's apple. He drops the needle and grasps his throat with his hand. As he tries to yell she stabs him in the shoulder. Gasping, he tries to reach for the syringe.

Again she thrusts the ball point pen into the side of his neck feeling it stick deep before pulling it out again. His blood gushes out in a crimson spray all over her hand and face making her scream in squeamish disgust. Then she thrusts the pen into his throat again. Bronson grasps at his gushing throat as she raises the pen and stabs him again, this time catching the back of his hand. He drops to his knees, clutching his throat, unable to make any distinguishable sounds. He gurgles as he raises a hand as if to stop her, his blood pooling around him as it sprays from the side and front of his neck to the rhythm of his heartbeat.

Gin stabs at him again with the pen, catching his hand again, where it pierces and goes through. She tries to pull it out, but it has lodged itself in his hand. She scrambles back from him as he holds onto his throat, one hand with a pen sticking through his palm, both soaked in his own blood. He wriggles around, making a couple more disgusting gurgling sounds before falling to his side on the floor. Within seconds he becomes motionless; his dark eyes staring blankly toward the wall. The colorful flowers on his shirt soak up crimson blood.

The voice's coarse whisper coaxes her, "Run Gin!" Gin quickly crawls to the syringe that has been dropped and then kicks at Bronson's lifeless body on the floor, to make sure he wasn't moving. She fumbles to get the keys from his pockets as her stomach churns from the blood that is soaking her. She removes the keys and stumbles back looking at his body, now surrounded by a huge pool of blood. She slips as she stumbles backward.

She jumps up and scurries to the door that is cracked open. Swinging the heavy door open the voice commands, "Go to the left. There's no one to the left." Gin runs barefoot with a syringe in one hand and the keys in the other as fast as she can out the door and to the left, down the hall past the patient doors that were sealed tight. She runs down the stairs at the end of the hallway toward the double doors as fast as she can, trying to catch her breath. She looks over her shoulder to see if she has been spotted, then fumbles with the keys to find the one that would open the doors.

After three tries she drops the keys with a loud jangle on the checkered floor. "Come on!" She yells to herself as she grabs the fallen key ring, "Come on. Come on." She shuffles to try another key. "YES!" The key slides into the lock and turns. She shoves open the door as she looks over her shoulder again.

Steve yells from behind her "Hey! Get back here!" He runs toward her as she slides through the door and pulls it closed behind her, hearing it latch. She finds herself in a stairwell that leads down. She bolts down the first set of stairs and around the corner before she can hear the guard at the door above her. He unlocks the door and she can hear his heavy stomping as he hurries toward her. "Get back here! Stop Gin!" he yells.

She rounds the corner and starts down the next set of stairs, then the next. She has no idea where she is going or how many floors there are but she keeps running, keys and syringe in hand. Her heart races as she runs as fast as she can down the stairs. She steps wrong on a stair and rolls her ankle, falling the rest of the way down the flight. She scrambles to get up as Steve is now on the flight of stairs just above her. She steps on her injured foot and almost falls again, leaving her in excruciating pain. "Oww." She forces herself to endure the pain as she goes down another flight of stairs using the rail to brace herself.

She nears the landing when the security door just below bursts open and two more guards appear. "Where do you think you're going?" one of them asks in a demanding tone. Gin looks up to see the guard nearing her.

Before she knows it, one of the two guards grabs her forcefully by the arm. She faces him and with all her might stabs the syringe into his arm. His grasp lets go as he slowly falls to the ground, eyes rolling into the back of his head. She turns to run, but a guard snatches her by the hair, yanking her back. She screams as she swings her arms around in defense. One of them tackles her to the floor face down as another grabs her wrists and pins them behind her back. "Oh no you don't." Steve says agitatedly.

She squirms, trying desperately to free herself as the guards and nurses hold her to the ground. "Let me go! No! Let me go!" She feels a stinging prick in her arm from a needle. "No!" she yells, "Let me go." Her voice trails as the floor grows blurry and she can no longer fight back. She goes limp as everything in front of her fades to black. The yelling swirls in vivid colors in front of her closed eyes.

Marie sits solemnly on the couch by herself. The chubby guy sits with his back to everyone staring at the TV; like usual.

Gin takes a seat next to Marie on the frumpy couch. She can see through the hair that hangs down the sides of her face, almost covering Marie's expression entirely. Her wrinkled frown is making her lower lip pout. Her stare is straight at the ground by her feet. Her shoulders are slightly forward and her hands are on her knees. She doesn't look up as Gin plops down beside her.

"What's wrong?" Gin looks under the side of her hair to see if there was a reaction or just one of Marie's staring spasms. After seeing her frown deepen she asks, "Are you okay?"

Marie shakes her head barely moving at all without saying a word. She sits motionless for a few moments before saying, "Annie just got back from treatment." She doesn't say anything else.

"Is everything okay, did something happen to her?"

Marie pulls her legs closer to her body. "She's fine." She raises a hand and moves the hair from part of her face revealing the stains of dried tears. "She's asleep."

"What's wrong?" Gin moves a little closer and in a hushed tone asks her, "What's wrong, you can tell you me."

Marie shakes her head, never removing her glazed stare from the floor. "I can't tell you how I feel." She shakes her head more.

Gin pushes, "Why are you so upset about Annie? What happened to her?"

Marie turns and looks at Gin with bloodshot eyes. Her eyes droop almost as far as her matching frown, then fill with brimming tears. "I know what it's like. I can't tell you what it's like."

Gin sits up straighter, "Oh my god, I'm sorry Marie. I can't imagine."

Marie snaps back, "No…No you can't." She wipes a tear with her hand as her hair and face fall back to the floor. "And you never should." She sniffles and continues, "They say it makes me better, but I feel like a part of me dies every time it happens." She sniffles again. "Every time they try to help me I feel like they rip away layers of my personality. We're slowly being turned into coin operated toys."

Gin tries to comfort her though she doesn't have a clue how. She feels horrible for her. She is looking at this normally tough girl turned into a frail shadow of the person she had been the day before.

Marie looks at her again. "I'm afraid that it's going to happen again. I can't do it again." Her tone is hushed as she looks around. "I have to a find way out of here. I have to."

Gin quietly responds as she looks around at the ignorant, blissfully delusional people in the room with them. "I know. We have to get out of here. Soon. There must be a way out."

Marie shakes her head. "I've tried."

"Me too." Gin adds.

Marie goes on, "This place is a huge maze. Some of the hallways just lead deeper into the Spookatorium."

Gin's face creases as she speaks. "What do you mean deeper?" Her stomach leaps into her throat.

Marie turns her face out of view behind her brunette hair. "Haven't you ever noticed that you can run and never go anywhere?! There are hallways that only spiral deeper into the gut of this hell hole."

Gin nods. "It is hard to figure out where you are once you're out of this ward. I thought I was close to an exit last time though. I know it. Damn Steve." She sighs heavily.

"Ha. Tell me about it. Even when I've slipped out without anyone seeing me, Steve somehow knows exactly where I am." She looks toward Gin, but not directly at her. "We would have a better chance if we work together. I don't want to see them catch you and fry your brain like they do mine."

Gin shudders at the thought. "We would most definitely be more likely to get the hell out of here if we can figure out how to get out fast enough. As undetected as possible."

"Yea."

"Next time either of us has a chance, we'll get the other and go for it then." She abruptly stops.

George approaches them with his shoulders drooping forward. "Gin do you want to watch a movie with me and Alfred?" He giggles in a shriek before continuing, "Sleepless in Seattle. It's supposed to be a great love story. You like love stories still right?"

Marie's irritated tone snaps like a whip at him. "No she doesn't want to watch some stupid lovey-dovey movie with you guys."

Gin replies, "Thanks George but I'm not going to watch any

movies tonight."

"Oh! You're up to sss-ssomethin'." He starts to get excited, which Gin knows means drawing attention to them.

"Shh. Shh. I'm not doing anything." She motions with her hands for him to calm down. "I'm just not really in a movie kinda mood tonight. Ya know what I mean?"

He nods his wrinkly chin. "I know what you mean. If you decided to watch it will you sit by us? We want to look our best for the new guy. If he is half as smart as his neat-o-nurse hair then damn we're in trouble."

Gin nods. "If I watch the movie I'll watch it with you."

"Okey dokey!" As quickly as he had appeared he is gone.

Marie, still irritated, snaps "Why in the world would he think we'd go out of our way to impress some stupid nurse?"

Gin doesn't hesitate to get back to working out a cooperative effort to figure out how to navigate the ridiculous amount of hallways in this building. She knows she was close. Her gut tells her that if she had made it a bit further she would have been out.

They discuss the places they have explored so far. Neither has made it outside so they plan a route to take next time that they agree seem most likely to be an actual way out.

They talk quietly until they are sent to their rooms by Steve.

Gin stares blankly at her ceiling wondering when she'll have the next chance to get out. She charts their idea and then thinks about it again. She knows that she won't have much time to think about it; she'll have to act and remember.

She restlessly slings her feet over the bed and sits at the desk. She stares at the box and holds it, running her fingers a crossed the edges. She opens its hinges. The stack of postcards were still arranged neatly. She strains in the dark to read the handwriting on the back of one. She has no idea who had sent them. She thought it was even stranger that these were supposed to be in her room. If they were ever hers, she certainly didn't get them through the mail; despite the post marked stamps. She feels the edges of the stamp on the surface of the smooth cards.

The words on them don't make sense. Who will see her soon? Why are there no names on the postcards? There were some from all over the country. Someone may have gone through a lot of trouble to make her feel crazy. She knows she isn't crazy; the one thing she knows for sure.

She can't stay here. They won't let her out. She knows that

with Marie's experience in here, there's a much higher chance she can get out. She falls asleep in the wee hours of the night with spiraling hallways mocking her to sleep.

16

Gin wakes up feeling a piercing pain in her shoulders as if she'd slept on them too long. She tries to readjust and is instantly aware she is restrained and has stressed her shoulders to the point of fatigue.

She is shaken from sleep but having difficulty holding her eyes open. She tosses her head side to side to shake the deep sleep she's been in. Her throat is sore from snoring; she is sure of it.

"No. No. Not again!" She twists like a rubber band to check if she's loosened anything in a previous attempt to free herself.

After brutally hurting her shoulders more, she realizes her defeat. She balls her fists in their padded cuffs. "You can't do this to me! Let me go. Just let me go!"   Anger washes across her face as she yells at the empty room, "God dammit let me the hell outta here."

She bites her lower lip and closes her eyes. This can't be happening to her. If they would stop pumping her liver full of drugs, she could clearly think about getting out of this hell hole of a prison. Again she yells, hoping someone will hear her. "What's going on? Why are you keeping me here?"

Gin looks toward the closed iron clad door. She feels rage building up, ready to bubble over. Her dehydrated lips press together. Her chest rises up before she huffs in an attempt to deal with the possibility that she can't free herself from them. There's no way to wriggle her way out of these cuffs and she knows that she can do more damage to herself. Her shoulders are throbbing from exhaustion.

She doesn't remember how she got here. She's not sure how she got tied up. How can she not remember it? How could this happen? Gin knows she can't trust anything they tell her. Again she screams, "You can't keep me here. You CAN NOT keep me tied up in here. Let me the fuck out!"

She moans as she moves her sore body in an effort to look around the cold and moldy room that imprisons her. On her side, the chair is neatly tucked under the desk. Her box is open; its hinged lid hung backwards. The post cards haphazardly peek out of the top.

She is certain that she had closed it tightly! Someone was messing with her things while they had her knocked out. They had to have been. This charade is relentless. "What the hell?"

Gin shakes her head as she thinks about how the complexity of her situation is worsening. They were trying to make her think she was crazy so she would play along with their games. This elaborate scheme to hold her and the others here against their will needed to be stopped. Has to be stopped. Joe will help her. He will take her away from this evil place of torture. If only she had some way to tell him where she is.

Joe will ensure they pay for what they've done to her. His charm and smooth talking ways would turn this into the tragedy of the century. He will use his status and power to publicize the horrid things that are going on to the people here. No court would ever think of letting such sadistic people roam the streets ever again.

She wants nothing more than to feel his strong comforting arms and see his sympathetic, understanding eyes looking back at her. Aloud she murmurs, "I will find you Joe. You have to know what they're doing to me…" Her voice fades, turning into stifled moans. Her eyes swell and a louder moan escapes her lips. "Help me. Please help me."

Gin lies restrained and medicated knowing that someone will be coming to make sure she is fully doped up again soon. She tries to clear her mind and think. There has to be something she's missed. If she could just clear her head of the fog, she could watch for careless mistakes and keep trying to remember the routes she's taken in this twisted penitentiary. What kind of merciless people would build a giant maze to keep people in?

The hinges on the door make a scratchy screech as they open. Ron Jon looks in on Gin with a smile. "Oh good. You're awake." He motions to someone in the hallway to come to him then turns back to Gin.

She looks toward the ceiling and in a monotone voice tells him, "I want you to let me out of here," She swallows hard and continues, "There are people that will find me. They won't rest until they find me." Her lip quivers and she locks her gaze on a tile on the ceiling. She concentrates on holding her lips still and not showing them her fears.

Ron Jon moves toward her casually, looking at her wrists then her ankles without touching them. "You need to relax Gin." He examines her ankles more intently. "Looks like you've been fighting instead of resting and you've hurt your ankles. Do they hurt?"

"How can you tell me to relax?!" She shoots words back at him, being careful not to let her go of her emotions. They can't know how scared she is. She is stronger than this. "The others may play along with your little game of risk, but I'm not convinced, not even a little." She shifts her gaze to his seemingly sincere smile. "Why am I being kept here? Is it money? Does this have something to do with Joe?"

Ron Jon repeats in a soft voice, "You need to relax Gin. No one is trying to harm you. You've had a rough day and need to get some rest."

Without blinking she replies, "Would you be calm if you were tied up against your will like this?"

Without hesitation he responds, "That all depends on the situation doesn't it." His bright eyes sparkle as he tries to gain her trust. "I need you to stay calm and really give yourself a break. You could really use a break from your anger and emotions. We can only help you so far."

Steve walks through the doorway and joins them, holding a large plastic cup. "I brought you water." He extends his arm to show her. She turns her head away.

Ron Jon coaxes her, "Drink Gin you have to get liquids. I'd hate for you to get dehydrated."

"Please don't pretend you actually care about me anymore."

Gin watches as Steve shifts his weight and rests his hand on one hip. Ron Jon's smile sinks and his eyebrows turn downward in the center. He squints observing her.

He gets closer and in a loud whisper says, "If you can't drink your liquids and manage to make yourself dehydrated, we WILL have to give you liquids in a tube. I don't want to see that happen to you again."

Gin shoot up as far as she can within her confines making Ron Jon jump and stumble backward. "What the hell do you mean 'again?' What the hell are you fucks trying to do here?" She jerks on her wrists and kicks her feet. "You don't have me fooled. Your big puppy-dog eyes and impeccable white smile don't fool me like your other ridiculous puppets out there." She glares at them as she continues, "Are they all a part of your elaborate plan too? Or?! Are they just like me, being held against their will?"

Steve moves closer to her and reaches around the back of her head. She yells and tosses her head around as if she could escape his grasp. He firmly grasps the back of her skull and lifts her head. She presses her lips together and squints her eyes. He carefully lifts the plastic cup to her face. "You have to drink now."

"I won't. You'll have to make me. Why doesn't anyone explain what's going on around here. Are you going to tell me I need to relax and heal?" Her sarcasm is met with as sharp of a glare at him. His eyes narrow and he wrinkles his cheeks into a fake smile. She pinches her dry lips together in defiance. She won't give in to them. She's not going to show them that she is afraid. After all, she's completely helpless in her current condition.

Steve's emotionless voice replies, "I don't want to make you Gin. I want you to drink it on your own."

She shakes her head in his large hand, staring fire into his eyes. She hopes he will explode. She doesn't care if the whole place blows up, exposing everyone here.

He lets go of her and turns to walk away. Ron Jon explains, sighing, "Gin you should have drank when you had the chance. We can't help you if you won't let us."

She snickers under her breath. "Huh, help me. You can't help me unless you're going to let me go. I have a feeling that's not why you're here." Her stare returns to the ceiling.

Steve shakes his head. "You know you can't leave Gin. The only way out is if the boss man says you can. We're not in charge of when you can do that."

She laughs, "Yea, you're not in charge. You're just here to

make sure I'm comfortably numb so you can torture me some more."

Ron Jon speaks up, "Hey now, we're not here to torture any-one." He flashes his famous perfect smile. She doesn't look at either of them or acknowledge that they're still in the room with her.

After pausing and waiting for her to react, Ron Jon motions to Steve and both men leave the room without another word. Gin silently frowns. She was incredibly thirsty, but there's no way she's giving into them. It may not have even been water.

The light flickers off and Gin lays in the dark. Her sniffles echo back at her. She feels so alone. She no longer has the strength to fight her bindings. Her homesick sobs fill the room until she is so exhausted that she can't stay awake anymore. No tears fall from her eyes; she's all out of tears. Her body relaxes as she falls into comfort-able sleep.

17

Gin lies silently on her bed, breathing heavily. Outside her room the hallway lights flicker and return to their dim illumination. She stares through the tiny window on the door to the light outside, without moving from her pillow.

"Wake up Gin. It's time to wake up." She sleepily rubs her eyes. Without opening her eyes she stretches with a yawn and props herself up.

Darkness surrounds her, hugging her like a warm blanket of comfort. She sits with her heavy legs dangling off the side of the bed; almost touching the floor. Her eyes slowly open and close while she touches her arms. Her shoulders still throb. Rubbing one shoulder with her fingertips, she manages to keep her eyes open, despite their need to slam shut. Her sleepy gaze drifts back to the little window on the door.

The ominous voice calls to her in its usual emotionless tone,

"It's time Gin."

Gin nods her head, moving her neck and shoulders in a rocking motion. She wipes at her eyes again and stands up as if placing every vertebra deliberately in place; one at a time. Gin carefully rises to a wobbly stand, using the bed for support for a moment.

"She's coming for you." There is a long pause and the deep voice continues, "You know what you have to do."

Gin steps slowly, her feet and toes crackling and popping as she dazedly steps on the cold floor toward the door.

"She'll be here soon. She's unarmed, but others will follow her to you." Gin stands behind the door, swaying and looking out the little window. There seemed to be nothing out there. Gin tries the handle. Locked. She blinks slowly, resting her back on the wall just beside the door.

She looks around the darkness. "Who's coming?" The room is so silent that she hears her heart. Looking around, her eyes adjust and she can see the chair arbitrarily shoved to the side of the desk. The box on top of it is closed. She can't tell if it's latched, but it isn't as she remembers it from the day before. Or was it this morning?

She stands resting on the wall for some time before she hears the muffled rustling of the door being unlocked. Clink-tonk. Gin is completely awake now. She feels her palms start to sweat as she waits for the door to open. It seems like an eternity that she waits, not sure exactly who is waiting for her on the other side.

The door unlocks and creaks open slightly as the light flickers on above. She hears the familiar jingle of keys and the screech of the medicine cart, then the door opens more.

Gin wrenches the door open from behind, catching Nurse Bettie completely off guard. Bettie drops her clipboard and clutches the door handle and pulls it partly closed as Gin tugs on the handle, working a hand into the crack of the door for a better grip. They struggle over the door for a moment before Gin slides a foot into the small opening.

Gaining control of the door the chubby woman yells, "Gin what are you doing?! You're supposed to be resting."

"I've been waiting for you." Gin squeezes her knee through and pushes the heavy door using her thigh. She busts through, throwing the door open and away from the nurse's grasp.

Nurse Bettie puts her chin down and looks at Gin with a menacing grin across her face. "You should be sleeping. After all, it's the middle of the night, child." She puts her hands firmly on her hips and finishes, "I will shove your medicine down that pretty little piehole if you don't get back in your room." She looks from side to side and smiles her smirk.

"I will not go back in there. I won't take any more of your dammed pills and I'm not going to let YOU fuck up my head any-more." Gin clenches her jaw and moves closer to the nurse, not taking her eyes off her.

Bettie quickly opens the sliding cabinet door and reaches inside, slightly bending at the knees. Gin lunges around the cart and kicks the nurse in the forearm as hard as she can without losing her balance. Wails of pain echo down the hall as the nurse yanks her fist out of the cart. "I knew you were going to make me do this."

Gin can see the gleam of a needle in her hand. Gin jumps toward her. She tries to get a good grasp as the nurse grabs her hair and tries to pull her toward the floor with one hand, while firmly holding the syringe with the other.

Both women struggle, and Gin pushes the nurse's arm away from her while trying to free her hair. Some of it rips from her skull. She lets out an angry snarl of a moan and tackles Nurse Bettie to the floor.

Her hair is freed as they both fall to the floor, sending the cart banging and rolling against the wall. She scrambles to push the needle away when the nurse stabs at her twice, nearly catching Gin in the shoulder. They roll around for a moment with the syringe stabbing madly toward Gin. She rams her palm square into the fat ladies nose, sending her head into the floor with a thud.

Stabbing again Nurse Bettie yells in a deeper, sterner voice, "I'm going to get you. You stupid little shit. You shouldn't have done that."

Barely dodging the needle and holding tight onto the nurse's wrist, Gin grits her teeth and pushes as she yells back "I won't let you hurt me anymore." She grunts deafeningly as the two roll around trying to gain control of the syringe. Gin reaches her arm up and grasps Bettie's throat which she uses to hold her weight on before being bucked off.

A gasp for air followed by Bettie's long snicker make Gin enraged. Bettie smashes the hand and knuckles that have a hold of her into the hard floor with a crack. Gin yelps in pain eight inches from the nurse's face. She knows she has to kill her. It's the only way out.

With another cackling laugh Bettie snidely hisses, "The others are coming. I'm going to make sure they take you away for good you little shit!" She grunts as her girth pushes Gin over onto the floor long enough to get back up to her knees. Her hands turn white and her round cheeks turn fire red.

Gin leaps toward the nurse again. The needle comes thrusting toward her. She feels the sting of it going into her bicep as she grasps Nurse Bettie's neck. "Ouch!" She yelps as the needle is pulled from her skin and stabbed a second time, right next to where it had gone before.

Gin holds onto the nurse's throat. She feels skin squeeze in-between her fingers as she squeezes as tightly as she can around her throat.

The syringe stabs Gin two more times, making her screech in pain. She squeezes tighter on her throat hold. Bettie turns bright red as she drops the needle and tries to pull Gin from her neck as she flops around to free herself. She claws at Gin's hands in an attempt to breathe. Her arms flail as she hits Gin in the face and neck as she struggles.

Gin pulls her face away from the flinging hands just after she catches a hit to the temple and then one to the forehead from the other hand. She immediately recoils in pain, almost losing her grip on the wiggling nurse.

Gin pushes with all her might, fighting to keep pressure on Bettie's neck.

The nurse hits Gin in the nose, causing it to drain blood down the back of her throat and down her lips. Gin's eyes burn and start to water. She feels blood roll down her chin. Her eyes are so blurry that she can't see the horrified look across her attackers face.

Bettie wails on her face with both hands so hard that Gin is pushed back. The nurse has time to gasp for air and try to get away. She scrambles to the cart as Gin clutches her own face and wipes it onto her shirt, smearing blood across her face. She huffs and charges the nurse whose hands are almost in the cart.

Gin tackles her, knowing that the only way out of this place is through her. She doesn't have a choice. She has to get out.

Bettie yells for Steve as she reaches into the cabinet and feverishly searches for something. Gin jumps on her back and sinks her teeth into her shoulder making her yell. Gin pulls Bettie away from the cart just as she sees the tingle of a needle rolling though pill bottles.

Gin feverishly rummages in the open door of the cart and grabs a tourniquet with the tips of her fingers. The nurse grabs her by the wrist. "You're not going to get away with this. When security gets here I will make sure you pay for this."

Gin instinctively punches her across the chin with her free

hand. She throws her arms at Bettie and wraps the tourniquet around the back of her neck as she is pushed away. "No I won't you bitch. You're going to pay for what you've done to all of us."

She crosses the ends and pulls with all her might, making Bettie fall to her knees as she scrapes at the restraint. The indentation it makes is impossible for her to get her hands underneath. Gin wraps it two more times, pinning one of her struggling hands under it on accident, but she likes the overall effect. She knots it and steps back.

The nurse twists and turns as she is strangled, finally falling over and wriggling. Gin laughs because she can almost say it was by her own hand.

She quickly scours the cart for any remaining weapons. She grabs a large glass bottle with liquid in it, a stethoscope, and an empty syringe. She grabs the items, looking back at Bettie's unmoving body. She searches pockets for keys. When she's got them and unhooks them from a string that is holding them in place, she runs as fast as she can toward Marie's room.

She fumbles to find a brass key to match Marie's door lock. On the third try she gets it. Clunk-tunk. It turns and she pushes the heavy door open. "Marie. Marie let's go!"

Marie jumps up and scrambles behind Gin. They run down the hallway to a set of doors. "Hurry." Marie coxes.

Gin unlocks the door, they round the corner and run as fast as they can. Their bare feet thud on the floor.

They push the doors open to the stairway and bolt down them almost in unison. Both girls have run this way before. They hear no signs of anyone from above, as they follow the stairs down toward the ground level. "One more!" Marie says through catching her breath.

Marie's hand reaches the door first and pulls it wide open as they continue into the darkness past it. They charge down the hallway and Marie stops for a moment in front of two doors. One on each side of the hall. "It's this one." She pushes the door with a small wired glass window on the left. It's locked.

Gin tries several keys, none fit. Marie looks both ways feverishly as she impatiently waits. Lights flicker then turn on from the direction they came from. Gin finds the key that fits after what seemed like a hundred tries. Her heart beating in her throat the whole time. They can hear yelling from a distance now.

The lights turn on above their heads in the hall, as the girls slip through the door into the darkened room, re-locking the door.

Windows with drawn curtains line both sides of the room, letting a little artificial light peek into the room. Marie leads the way through the room. "I know we're almost there. This is the way out!" They hear yelling as security is on their tracks and banging on the door two-hundred feet behind them.

"Here." Gin hands Marie the keys as she looks around the dimly lit space. "This could be the way out." Her voice is excited, even through the panic. They seem to be in an office area that clearly isn't used at night.

They come to a locked door on the end of the long room and Marie, expertly it seems, gets it on the second try. "This has to be it!"

Both girls gasp as they smell fresh cold air in their faces. Marie pulls the keys out as they both excitedly step out onto cold, wet concrete. They door closes by itself with a dainty click. "RUN." She urges Marie even though they can't see more than ten feet from her face.

They run down what seems like a sidewalk away from the building. Gin ignores the piercing cold in her nostrils as she runs. She looks back as she hears Steve's familiar Voice. "Out here! Outside. Get the lights!"

Suddenly, lights on either side of the girls turn on with a blazing orange glow. Both of them stop dead in their tracks.

Marie angrily starts to yell "no" repeatedly, but Gin can't hear her. She spins around and grasps the syringe tightly. "Here." She mutters the words and extends the syringe to Marie.

They are in a courtyard. The only way out is the way they came in. A giant courtyard to nowhere. The walls are tall and stone. Gin grasps the stethoscope she has under her arm.

The glass jar slips from her sweaty palm as she feels rage boil inside her. They both jump as the glass shatters around them, nearly missing both of their bare feet. They yell, startled, and try to get away from the shards.

The sound of the men on the other side of the door gets louder as both girls try to get away from the glass without being cut.

The door opens in slow motion as Gin hears Steve yell. The words are a blur. Gin and Marie look at each other, both with the same instinctive gleam and with a nod lunge toward the three men.

Gin hears Marie yell out as she stabs an orderly with the needle. She can hear grunts and yelling all around her. She pulls her arm back and strikes Steve on the face, inches from an existing, healing cut. The stethoscope lashes him like a whip. She screams as she recoils and strikes him a second time, this time near his nose with the metal tip of the stethoscope. She feels a sharp pain from impact on her shoulder as she falls to the hard ground. As she falls, she sees a bloody orderly pinning Marie face down and shouting. Gin's head hits the ground as she watches Marie sedated by Ron Jon.

Her head spins as she feels flashes of colors in front of her eyes as her head contacts the hard concrete. She struggles to get her hands underneath herself. Hands grab her wrists and force her onto her face as she feels the familiar sting of a needle in her arm.

She wriggles for a moment before the muffled yelling fades into the calm darkness she is slipping into.

Gin is awakened by a throb on the side of her head. She pulls her hands up as a flood of tears swell in her eyes. She opens her eyes and confirms that she's back in her cell. She can't help but let out a cry as she kicks at her bed in frustration.

After several minutes she sits up, her hair splayed around her face. Rubbing her head, she sees a pile of papers setting on the little desk next to the box.

Jumping up, she grabs the papers and inspects the stapled bundle. She flips the blank first page. It's Marie's Journal! How did it get in here? It's at least sixty pages long.

Gin's eyes scan the hand-written pages. Each one is filled with words, front and back. She thumbs through the pages feeling guilty for looking through her friend's personal journal. Her eyes stop on the bold scribbled writing on one of the pages.

"…so much blood. Caroline's tears weren't tears anymore. They are blood soaked memories of a time before she was ripped from me. "

Trembling Gin tosses the whole thing back on the desk. She shudders as the words echo through her head. She shouldn't be looking at this. She sits back on the bed and rocks herself. She gets up and tries the door. It moves and she re-closes it.

Gin paces around the room then returns to the bed. She spends several minutes sitting on the bed staring at the pages on the desk. Curiosity eats at her. She knows how upset Marie gets when talking about what happened. She chews on the side of a fingernail eyes glued to the papers.

Her friend wouldn't have to tell her if she just looked at a little of it. She didn't though, instead she hops up and goes back to the door. She pulls it open and heads toward the common room. She peers into the room. Only Alfred is there, sitting quietly sipping on his tea.

Spotting Gin he waves to her. "Good morning Gin." She waves back.

Gin steps closer to him. Her voice trembling as she asks, "Have you seen Marie yet today?"

A puzzled, loony look crosses his face. "No, I'm sorry Gin.

Maybe your Marie is in an intake meeting?" he sips his tea with a pinkie finger hovering slightly above his cup. "Seems like those take a while."

"Intake meeting? Intake where?" Gin's confusion makes Alfred set his cup down.

He looks at her and tilts his head. "Nurse Bettie and the Doctor usually take about four hours with all the talky talking they do."

Gin turns to head back to her room. "Okay Alfred. Thanks." She shakes her head and rolls her eyes as she adds, "Tell her to find me if she comes in okay?"

"I will tell her, should I see her."

Gin looks down the hallway at the closed doors. Marie's door is too far away to tell if it's open or not. Maybe Alfred made sense today and she had some kind of meeting. She goes back to her room and closes the door. She rushes to the bound pages and sits down as she thumbs through them. She stops on a random page.

"The yelling had to stop. His gurgles angered me and all the days he spent hitting mother had to be stopped. Even with the side of his mouth smashed off, he still thought he could yell at me."

Gin sits straighter as she closes the pages quickly. She sighs heavily, shaking her head. She isn't sure she wants to know anymore. As if daring herself, she flips to halfway through the stack of pages.

"The cart was all I had, but it was more than enough to make his face look like clay. That stupid grin he had was washed all over the side of the metal."

Gin again slams the dream journal shut. How could Marie know about that? How could another so-called patient find out about that? No one had seen it. Wouldn't Marie have brought it up if she had been outside her door but gone before she tried to escape? Puzzled, she puts the journal back on the desk. Why didn't she help me if she was there? Why was her journal in her room at all?!

She rubs her head as she lays down and pulls the covers over her head. She breaths her hot moist breath. She is very tired and the pages don't make any sense. She'll ask Marie about it after she gets up for the day, or gets done with Dr. Veinkman.

Gin dozes off thinking of the night before and the puzzling pages that sit on her desk. She also thinks about the fact that she might have a concussion. Sleep just seems so comforting right now. Just for a minute.

She fades in and out between sleep and startling herself awake for a couple hours. She eventually sits up and looks at the journal, still sitting on the desk.

19

Gin knows she has to be most of the way through the four hours before Marie will be back. She needs to know why this journal existed. How could this be the diary Marie writes in? There are things that were written one day a time; one sheet a day. Gin thought only she knew about the nurse. She has to hurry and read more before she got back.

She flipped the page.

...I remember beating her senseless with a book. Not just for learning anymore. I don't know why she was so defenseless against that stupid fucking book. I stopped her from hurting me though. That voice has become like home. He told me to be quick and I was quick. I didn't even give them a chance...

Gin shivers at the thought and flips several pages.

...That stupid man-nurse, he was going to get me

like the others, but I had an edge on them. I was told he was sneaky and not to trust him. He needed more than his needle just to take me away. I know they know how, but I don't let them…

She turns the page again. How could this be happening? She remembers being there! It hadn't been someone's dream! She had been there. That exact thing.

…was so stupid in his Hawaiian getup. He tried to kill me with pills. Those weren't my pills. HE told me they were going to try again. Damn nurse's head smashed like a melon…

Gin fumbles and drops the journal on the floor. She can hear her heart as she tries to pick up a couple pages that had fallen out. She knows doesn't have time to read the whole thing. She scans a page as she picks the others up.

…I hitch-hiked to some crappy Motel and found Mark working the late shift. I instantly knew what he wanted and I rode that cowboy most of the night. My sweet one had warned me that that bastard would call the police when I wasn't looking. I knew I had to get him off me. He claimed to not know who I was, but since he did now, I had to shut him up…

Gin scrambles to put the pages back together and lays them back on the little desk. She silently backs out of her room and down the hall to the common room. She doubts anyone noticed she was gone.

How could the pages of that Dream Journal be explained? She sits on the edge of a couch and chews on the side of her finger.

Alfred stands gazing at some unknown beauty out the window.

"Hey Alfred, have you seen Marie lately?" Gin looks at him in his royal blue robe while still biting on the sides of her fingers.

He scratches his chin and walks closer. "I'm sorry dear. I don't believe that I know this Marie."

Gin rolls her eyes. "Come on, you know Marie." She raise her shoulders and wrinkles her nose. "She's usually sitting on the couch." Her tone was coarse and she was getting impatient.

He shrugs his shoulders and shakes his head. A frown crossed his lips. "Banana gram." He scratches his chin some more. "Perhaps you're looking for Annie or George."

Gin turns her back to him with a huff, making the couch

creak. She crosses her arms. "Are you kidding me? I don't have time for this today." She says to herself under her breath.

George sits at a table behind her winding string through his fingers. She knows he is mesmerized. "Hey George…" he looks up briefly. "Have you seen Marie today?"

George's eyes look as though they could pop out at any minute. "I'm George."

"Yea… George have you seen Marie?"

He sits, thinking hard. His tongue sticks out slightly as he sets the string aside to concentrate fully on what she'd asked. "There's no Marie. Only Gin."

Her irritation was obvious, "What the hell George. Not you too."

George starts clapping. "Oh. You said Marie. NO, no Marie."

Gin grows more frustrated. "What is wrong with you guys today? Don't pretend you don't know what I'm talking about."

Alfred goes back to the window as he adds, "I wish I could help you with your troubles, but there is no Marie my dear."

Gin storms to the office window and pounds on the glass of the half wall. Steve comes out the office door to the window. "What now Gin?"

She tries to remain calm. "Where's Marie today? I haven't seen her in a while and she was supposed to be back by now."

He looks her up and down with a blank expression. "Gin, there's no Marie here."

Gin's eyes show her shock. "What…where has she gone? What did you do to her?"

Gin knows Steve does not like her demanding tone, but sighs and says sternly. "Gin, there has never been a Marie here. Should I get the doc?"

She freezes in horror. How could they play this kind of trick on her? Of course there's a Marie. She was here a few hours ago at group…Or was it last night? No, it must have been yesterday.

She runs up the stairs toward the hall and then down the hallway to Marie's room. Steve yells up behind her. "I'm gonna call the Doc!"

A closed closet door stands where Marie's metal door should be. She looks up and down the hall before trying the locked handle. She pounds on the door. How can this be?!? I was just here, she thinks. She takes several steps to the left and counts the doors to the end. She looks at the numbers. 180, 181, 182, 183, 184. Closet. What the fuck is this?!?

How could this be? What is going on with the numbers? She grabs the handle on the door with both hands and pulls. "No, No. Marie…" Gin fights back the steaming tears in her eyes. "They can't take you away."

20

Gin runs down the hall to her room, unsure how she can even explain how freaked out she is. She pulls her door closed and sits on the bed, rocking herself slowly.

Out of the corner of her eye she notices her box is missing. The pages are gone too. She shoots over to the tiny table and searches for the box.

"It's gone." She runs her hand over the surface of the desk then looks underneath. She sees a familiar stack of papers. Marie's dream journal! Her box is on its side in the corner of the room, past the desk. "What's going on? Who's playing tricks on me? Why are you doing this?!?"

The room remains quiet as Gin clutches the corner of the neatly stacked Journal. She shakes it over her head and yells. "Where are you!?! What's going on here? What the hell is going on here? Marie...Oh Marie where are you?"

She sits back down on her bed, shaking. She refuses to look at the journal's pages. Warm salty tears are now streaming down her cheeks.

Ron Jon appears at the door. "Come on Gin, let's go see Dr. Veinkman." He gives her a warm smile before opening the door completely. Behind the door stands Steve, a look of concern across his face, large arms crossed.

Gin looks at them, then slowly looks back at the hand written journal. She gets up and follows them silently, her gaze fixed. She remembers how they screamed. She hadn't thought of it until now, but she remembers. The blood was gone. The voice seems to always warn her, otherwise she feels perfectly safe. They aren't here. None of them are here anymore. All the nurses are gone now. She remembers it.

Gin walks down the hall with her shoulders slouched forward and lost in her own thoughts of disbelief and despair. Where was Marie? Did they make her go away like Luke? She was the only friend she had in here.

Ron Jon leads her to the doorway of the office and motions for her to enter, while giving her one of his famous winks. "Go on in. He's waitin' on ya."

Gin nods and enters the large office. She clutches the journal with her knuckles turning white. Lines of worry swim across her face as she hardly notices the door close behind her.

Dr. Veinkman stands by the window looking at her with his round cheeks and pin stripes. The window is streaked with rain from a midday shower behind him. He warmly welcomes her. "Gin you needed to see me?"

She nods as she continues to frown. She holds out the journal. "What is this?"

He put his hands together and walks the tips of them back and forth a couple times before rubbing his chin and calmly replying, "That's your dream journal. You've written in one for many years."

She flings the journal around in the air in front of her face while shaking her head. Her face is full of worry. He must be lying to her!

"This is Marie's journal. How can this be my journal? Where is she?" She turns and looks at the Doc while she takes some deep breaths, trying not to let the sickness in her stomach take over.

He nods at her, "There is no Marie. You've made her up in your subconscious. You've been going through bouts of lucidity and healing with bouts of imagining a world in your sleep for years."

"No!" Gin's voice gets stern, "I won't believe that she's never been here. I won't! I did NOT make up Marie!" She huffs. "Did you make her go away like Luke?!? Is that what this is?"

His eyes show concern. "There isn't a Luke either Gin. There hasn't been a Luke in your ward as long as I can remember. I know this is hard for you."

The doctor looks at the wide-mouthed Gin with worry. "You are Marie. She is part of you. Your name is Jennifer Marie. This is part of how you cope with the traumas you've been through."

"No, that's not possible. I'm not supposed to be here. I need to call Joe. Let me call him." Gin pleads with the doctor. Her eyes and face form a deep frown.

"The boyfriend you met online while working at the bookstore?"

Gin wonders how he could have known any kind of details. She hasn't ever told anyone but Marie about meeting him online. "How'd you? Wait…"

He shakes his head. "There's no easy way to tell you this I'm afraid."

"What are you talking about?" She shakes her head in frustration. What is he doing? What is going on?

He shakes his head again as he remains calm and in a sooth-ing voice says, "You watched 'You've Got Mail' with George the first night you were in this ward. You've taken on the life of the main character ever since."

"What are you talking about? You've Got Mail?!? That's ri-diculous. That's a horrid movie."

"Is it now? You own a little bookstore that your mother strug-gled to keep open when she was alive. You worked there your whole life."

"What?" She musters the words out as she stumbles to one of the upholstered chairs. Gin throws herself into it as she shakes her head in disbelief. She sees spots as blood rushes behind her eyes.

"You are actually Gin, who is a very lost girl. You write your dreams down on the one sheet of paper you're given. Lately you've believed you're a fictional character in a movie."

Gin thumbs through the journal still cemented in her hand. "No, I remember Marie. She told me things. She's been here for a long time."

Dr. Veinkman crosses his arms around his round stomach.

"You've been in a ward since you were 15. You were just released from high security to here. You know many of the people here."

Gin looks at him in fear of his next words as she fights the urge to hurl up the contents of her stomach. "Fifteen, that's not possible." She nervously pushes the hair out of her face and behind her ears as she speaks, "I don't live here."

"Marie has been your imaginary friend for over seventeen years. You go in and out of remembering where you are and taking on a life that's easier. The last several dozen times it was from movies." He smiles. "You were told many years ago that if you wrote about the things you dreamed about it was better than if you acted on them. You've been writing religiously on one of those sheets, starting a couple years into your treatment, every day. Ingenious advice from a friend of mine on Ward 3."

Gin sits quietly in the chair, arms forward and neck hung low. "Are you trying to tell me that my life is a lie?" She sniffles.

He taps her on the shoulder trying to comfort her. "You have been coping with what happened to you in your own ways for a very long time now. Your life is not a lie. In fact, I'd say you're getting so much closer to getting healed. Better than ever."

Gin sobs out, "Why am I here? What's happening to me?"

206

The doctor walks over to the window, watching the rain drip down it and the lights from the lightning flicker. "You're here to allow yourself to heal. You're remembering the past that your subconscious has tried to protect you from. We've been working for many years together to get you through this."

Gin shakes her head and balls her fists, dropping the journal from her lap. "You mean Marie has never been here?"

He shakes his head. "No, she hasn't." He clears his throat before continuing, "Think about if you remember anyone else talking to her, or if it was always just you."

Gin thinks about group and Marie's snide comments. No one else had spoken to her. She was never called on. She thought about sitting in the common room and talking to Alfred and George. They hadn't talked to her either. Even the nurses and Steve had only spoken to her. That's just not possible. Her head was spinning out of control as scenes play in her head that Marie hadn't ever actually been in. But she had been right there; her friend.

The doctor clears his throat again and warmly continues, "You had an accident when you were fifteen. You've been having horrendous nightmares since. You've been deemed by the state to not be a harm to yourself or anyone else here, so you're here in Medium Security."

Gin rubs her temples and squints. "You mean to tell me that ALL the things Marie told me…happened to me?"

Dr. Veinkman nods his head slowly. "I don't know what you came up with, but you and your best friend were attacked by a young friend of yours. You got out of the situation by pure instinct. No child should have had to go through what you did, it's true. You had snapped something in that little lost head though and you didn't stop there. You killed your abusive father and didn't know where you were by the time you were found."

Gin gasps and covers her mouth. "I remember. I remember Dale. What about Dale? I remember him attacking me. I killed him. What about Nurse Bettie?" She looks up at the doctor who shakes his head with concerned look.

He answers, "You didn't hurt them, you dreamt it." He reaches down and picks up the Dream Journal from the floor. "It's all right here. It always has been. Dale got transferred to a different ward. We got the talented Ron Jon out of the transfer." He smiles, "Nurse Bettie is on a much needed vacation." He laughs a bit at the thought of how much she needed a vacation.

Gin feels like her world is swirling around. "Vacation?" Her voice is trembling as she speaks, "Nurse Bettie is on vacation?"

"That's right. She's been gone almost a week now, due back any day. Went to see her family in the South."

Gin shakes uncontrollably in the chair, trying to comprehend what she is hearing. "What about Nurse Bronson? I remember what happened to him…I remember."

The doctor walks around in front of her. He shakes the journal before tossing it onto his desk. "It's all in there Gin. Bronson is sick, has been for over a week now. Highly contagious." He walks to the intercom on his desk and presses a button. It beeps before he speaks into it. "Ron Jon can you please get Gin's box for me?

Over the loud speaker Ron Jon replies, "Yes. Right away sir."

The doctor presses the button again, "Thank you." He returns his attention to her. "Do you know how long you've been in this ward?"

She wipes her nose on the back of her hand. "A couple weeks?"

He frowns slightly, "No, Gin you've been in this ward for six weeks now. You've spent a bit of it staring into space, but you've always had trouble with time. That's nothing new."

Gin shakes her head. "Staring? No that was Marie. Luke said

she does it all the time…"

Dr. Veinkman walks back to the window and quietly replies, "Marie is you, Gin."

21

Her head is spinning as she sits in the doctor's office chair. How can this all be possible? She remembers so vividly talking to Marie just yesterday. How can she have made up a whole person? She remembers how many times the last few days that she'd sat with Marie. She'd really been sitting alone? That isn't possible!

This doesn't make any sense. She sits, taking deep, calming breaths as she tries to calm herself and take it all in. She doesn't know how much more her brain can take right now. She feels herself panicking as her heart and brain fight over her sanity.

A knock on the door is followed by Ron Jon, carrying a white file box, balanced on one arm as he struggles to close the door with the other. He quietly sets the box beside the desk before turning to leave without saying a word. Gin watches as he leaves, giving her a quick smile before closing the door behind him as the Doctor thanks him.

Dr. Veinkman turns the box so Gin can read the name on the side. Jennifer Marie Sterling. He opens the lid and pulls out a few stacks of paper, placing them in front of her on the desk. "It's all here Gin. Years of writing."

She sits on the edge of her seat and peers at the papers. Then she hesitantly reaches out and moves them around so she can read the covers. One has Dream Journal by Jennifer Marie Sterling written across the front in fat black marker. She sees one with the year 1995 then another date of 2015. She thumbs through the journals. They all have her handwriting and one sheet has been written on at a time. "How can this be? How could I NOT remember any of this?!"

Dr. Veinkman sighs as he explains, "There are times when you do try to leave. You kinda just wander off... Other times you want to get out. You and George were notorious for mischief a few years ago. You HAVE put up quite a fight in the past. You've been in high-security wards for well over twenty years." He chuckles again. "We've had no choice but to sedate you when you're really confused or even restrain you when our staff could be in danger. You are usually more of a danger to yourself than to the staff. Surely you can understand that Gin."

He straightens his tie. "There have only been a handful of times since your transfer where you've gotten out of hand. You've

214

even perfected getting out of normal restraints. It's a great thing they're not needed much these days. That means for ninety-five percent of the time you've been quite pleasant to be around." Gin swallows hard. "I know we're on the right path here."

A light knock on the door is answered by the doctor. He retrieves another box from Ron Jon, thanking him again. Dr. Veinkman places the little wooden box on his desk in front of Gin. Gin's eyes open wider. "My box!"

Dr. Veinkman opens the cherry box and pulls out several postcards. "These transferred with you. You have very few belongings and we make sure your box follows you." Gin takes a handful of cards from him hesitantly. She looks at the writing. They were all addressed to her. See you soon. Love Caroline. Her jaw drops as she looks at another one, then another. They were all from Caroline, sent to her childhood home. She sees them. They feel like they're burning holes in her palms as she reads then re-reads them.

Gin rubs her head as she sits on the chair. Caroline had always loved to travel and ALWAYS sent her a postcard. She pulls her hands through her hair to cover her face as she starts rocking herself slowly. The cards scatter around her.

She starts to remember Caroline and riding bikes through

the streets. Gin feels nausea kick in and holds her hand to her mouth. The doctor swoops in with a trash can. She closes her eyes as she remembers Caroline's last day. Gin throws up in the wastebasket she has gripped between her knees. She holds her hair to the side and sobs and vomits for what seems like forever.

Gin sits up and blows her nose, tossing it too into the trash. After wiping her eyes on another tissue, she sets the can down beside her and squints her eyes. She clenches her jaw as her lips quiver.

The doctor maintains his spot by the window. "Apparently, you're coming to terms with the reality of the reason we should continue your treatment," he gives her a thumbs up and a warm smile, "you should be so proud of yourself. You're on the right road to complete recovery and healing. It's true you shouldn't have been through what you have. Our job now is to make sure you can live a rewarding and fulfilling life."

She stands up straighter and rolls her shoulders around while taking a few calming deep breaths. She tries to erase the sight of Caroline struggling to get away from Ken. And the blood. So much blood.

The doctor rubs his chin with another look of concern. "You haven't let yourself realize what happened to you. All these years you've slipped into a dream world; someone else's story. You've made great progress in knowing the difference between your dreams and reality. You've written about the voices that tell you when to act nearly every day. You've seemed to know you were dreaming for years now. That wasn't always the case, of course."

All Gin can muster comes out is a soft whisper, "Caroline. I remember Caroline."

His voice is calm and soothing, "You should get some rest. We can talk about it more tomorrow after you've gotten some nice sleep tonight. I'll understand if you don't feel like contributing much in group tonight."

Gin nods her head. She has too many things to settle in her mind. She must be going crazy. This place is finally making her crack. She's not sure she can hold herself together much longer.

22

Gin sits on her bed. She's not sure how she got back to her room. She must have wandered back in a daze. There's so much time that she can't account for. She has no idea where it went. The last thing she knew she was talking with the doctor.

There's so much to take in. How could she let this happen to herself? What about her boyfriend? How could Joe just be a dream too?! She can almost feel his hand on her skin. She couldn't have imagined him too! She feels burning tears in the corners of her eyes as she realizes how alone she is. There may not be anyone trying to find her at all. No one waiting for her. Shivers cross her spine.

She lies on her side, resting her head on a hand. She thinks about the post cards. She remembers Caroline's smile and the hug she gave her when she left on another trip with her parents. She was always excited to come home and Gin was always waiting for her to hear all about the wonderful places she'd visited. Caroline always sent her a post card while she was gone. Always. She felt it was the least she could do, since she couldn't go too.

Gin's body shakes uncontrollably as her heart aches at the loss of her best friend. She's lonely and confused. She doesn't want to be here by herself like this. The friends she had are gone. They were never anything other than something she made up to keep herself occupied. The doctor said that she had made up elaborate lives to avoid her own memories. She wonders how often this happens. Her real memories have been sinking in more frequently… so she is getting better?!?

Waves of memories flood in as she recalls the last time she saw her friend. The day she was brutally taken from the world. They had been planning for weeks to work on their school project. They both had been researching and were sure they were going to get a good grade. They made a great team.

They had been sitting at the table waiting for Mike to come take them to diner when he and Ken were done being punks.

Ken had walked into Caroline's kitchen and wiped his palms on his jeans repeatedly as he tried to explain why Mike wasn't with him. At first, both girls thought he was joking. Mike and Ken had gone into the building together. He explained that he had gone inside, but came back out, leaving Mike inside. He heard someone coming and called to Mike to hurry up.

Ken said he left without him and he was sure that Mike wouldn't be coming after him anytime soon. Something about the way he explained it made her unsettled. Even now, hearing the words echo in her head, make her uneasy.

Gin pounds her fists on the bed beside her as the gruesome movie plays in her head. She watches again as Caroline fights with Ken and screams that he must do something. Why didn't he go back for him? Why wouldn't he help him?

Ken yelled at them that he wished he hadn't come back to tell us. He just wanted Caroline to know. As soon as the girls had wanted to find someone to help their friend Mike snapped and went into a rage.

Gin remembers Caroline reaching for help and screaming a blood curdling scream of pain as she hit the floor with Ken on top of her. Her arms reached out for anything she could find.

He slashed her so many times. Blood sprayed on the walls and on Gin. She had been covered in her own best friend's blood. She tried to help her friend. There was nothing she could do to stop him from killing her. She knew he would kill her too if she let him.

She remembers watching helplessly as the last bit of life left

Caroline's eyes. She had died at Gin's feet by the hand of a supposed friend of them both. Gin remembers the fear that consumed her as she sprang from the floor after Ken.

Before she knew it, she had been cut severely and Ken laid in a pool of his own blood, practically on top of Caroline. Adrenaline pumped through her veins. She had rolled him off of Caroline as his throat still gurgled.

She held her mutilated friend and screamed in agony, rocking her and telling her it's alright. She cried, tears drenching her face and dripping down on Caroline's blank face. She had moved all the hair from her face and kissed Caroline's forehead.

She had gotten up and picked up a cast iron pan that was on the stove. She slammed the pan over Ken's face with a crack. Again she raised the heavy pan and smashed his face. When the gurgling stopped and she was sure he was completely dead she spat on him and continued to yell and beat his body with the pan. Pieces of his skull and face had splattered on her and her clothes as she madly wailed on him.

Gin feels her head spin as she sees her concrete walls. She can't turn it off. It's too much for her. She shakes her head on her pillow yelling, "NO! No No no no. Caroline!" She sobs as she shakes her head in disbelief. "I'm so sorry I couldn't help you. Oh my god! I'm so sorry!"

Waves of nausea hit her, making her stomach flop. All she can see is Caroline's bloody body in her arms. She sits up just in time to lean over the side of the bed and throw up. She wipes her eyes and brushes her long hair behind her shoulders. Her stomach heaves again all over the floor.

The more it sinks in, the sicker she becomes. Her situation is terrifying and she's completely stuck here. There is no Joe going to rescue her. Her ears ring as she vomits repeatedly to the point of dry heaves. Her vision is blurred by tears and her nose burns as she fights the nausea.

Ron Jon and Steve stand at the door, watching her hurl and gasp for breath between loud sobs of misery. They both look at her with sullen faces. Steve speaks up when she begins to calm down a bit. "Gin, everything's going to be alright. Let's get you cleaned up so you can join everyone in group in a little bit."

Gin doesn't look at him but replies, "I can't. I just can't."

Ron Jon calmly says, "We have to take you Gin. I realize you could use some rest, but all you have to do is make it through group and you can relax for the rest of the evening. You'll have lots of opportunity to rest then. Come on, I'll take you to the bathroom so you can clean yourself up."

Gin looks at them with red swollen eyes. Without a word she stands and robotically walks out of the room. Turning back she shakily says, "There's a mess in there."

Steve nods. "It's alright, we'll take care of it. You'll have a fresh room by the time you get back from therapy."

23

Gin sits in her plastic chair in group therapy. George talks at her while she stares into space, breathing shallowly. The doctor walks in and takes his seat among the dozen patients. Steve follows him and closes the door, taking his statuesque pose.

George stands up and waves his arms around in a panic of excitement then sits back down. Gin never looks up.

Dr. Veinkman starts asking everyone how they are doing and if there's any news to report for the day. He asks several people, including Annie and Alfred if they've had anything exciting go on for the day. George stands and claps again.

The doctor calls on Gin. "Gin. Are you here Gin?" She doesn't reply but stares blankly and unblinking at the floor by her feet. She has no idea anyone is talking to her. "Alright then, we'll come back to Gin in a little while, she's had a rough day."

He turns to George. "George how are you today?" He clasps

his fingers together and looks at him.

George giggles and thwacks his palms together. "I'm soo so happy to have my Gin back." The room agrees and a few people clap. "Can we please never watch that nasty movie again Doc? Please please PLEASE?" He crosses his finger as he waits for an answer.

Dr. Veinkman chuckles. "I think we've all had enough of that particular movie. He looks at Gin, still completely unaware of her surroundings. "Let us never speak of it again."